PUFFIN BOOKS

Stealing the
Show

Luke Jennings is the author of three novels, including the Booker Prize-nominated *Atlantic*. His memoir, *Blood Knots*, was shortlisted for the Samuel Johnson and William Hill prizes. Before becoming a writer, Luke trained as a dancer and worked with classical and contemporary companies for ten years. He is currently the dance critic at the *Observer*, and has also written for *Vanity Fair* and the *New Yorker*.

You're less likely to know his daughter, Laura Jennings, who is thirteen and lives with her parents, two brothers and her dog Dusty. She says, 'At school I'm quite sporty but I like drama best, because I have always enjoyed acting, singing and performing. I love books, and my favourite author is Stephen King.'

Books by Laura and Luke Jennings

STARS

STARS: STEALING THE SHOW

Stars

Stealing the Show

LAURA & LUKE JENNINGS

PUFFIN

PUFFIN BOOKS

Published by the Penguin Group
Penguin Books Ltd, 80 Strand, London WC2R ORL, England
Penguin Group (USA) Inc., 375 Hudson Street, New York, New York 10014, USA
Penguin Group (Canada), 90 Eglinton Avenue East, Suite 700, Toronto, Ontario, Canada M4P 2Y3
(a division of Pearson Penguin Canada Inc.)
Penguin Ireland, 25 St Stephen's Green, Dublin 2, Ireland (a division of Penguin Books Ltd)
Penguin Group (Australia), 707 Collins Street, Melbourne, Victoria 3008, Australia
(a division of Pearson Australia Group Pty Ltd)
Penguin Books India Pvt Ltd, 11 Community Centre, Panchsheel Park, New Delhi – 110 017, India
Penguin Group (NZ), 67 Apollo Drive, Rosedale, Auckland 0632, New Zealand
(a division of Pearson New Zealand Ltd)
Penguin Books (South Africa) (Pty) Ltd, Block D, Rosebank Office Park,
181 Jan Smuts Avenue, Parktown North, Gauteng 2193, South Africa

Penguin Books Ltd, Registered Offices: 80 Strand, London WC2R ORL, England

puffinbooks.com

First published 2013
001

Text copyright © Laura and Luke Jennings, 2013
All rights reserved

The moral right of the authors has been asserted

Set in 13.5/16pt Baskerville MT Std
Typeset by Jouve (UK), Milton Keynes
Printed in Great Britain by Clays Ltd, St Ives plc

British Library Cataloguing in Publication Data
A CIP catalogue record for this book is available from the British Library

ISBN: 978-0-141-34443-0

www.greenpenguin.co.uk

MIX
Paper from
responsible sources
FSC
www.fsc.org   FSC® C018179

Penguin Books is committed to a sustainable
future for our business, our readers and our planet.
This book is made from Forest Stewardship
Council™ certified paper.

ALWAYS LEARNING   **PEARSON**

For Basil and Rafe

Late-afternoon sunshine lit the school grounds as Jessica Bailey hauled her suitcase across the drive towards the girls' dormitory block. Around her, other students were pulling their luggage from cars, blowing kisses to parents, waving goodbyes.

'Well, that's summer over,' said a voice behind her.

Jess swung round. 'Foxy!' she yelped, dropping her case. The two girls hugged. 'How *are* you? Wow, you look . . .'

And Eleanor Fox, as usual, did look amazing, the red cascade of her hair clashing spectacularly with her pink mohair coat. 'So how was your holiday?' she asked. 'Lots of glam parties, super-fit guys . . .'

'Not too many of either,' admitted Jess. 'Although the boy from my aunt's pet shop did try to snog me when we were cleaning out the hamster cages.'

'Try to?'

'Well, he was nice, but he smelt just a bit too much of gravy-flavoured dog chews.'

'Ew!'

'So what about you, Foxy? How was the south of France?'

'Weird, as usual! Dad on his BlackBerry by the pool, turning bright pink; Mum freaking out because they'd asked too many people to stay . . .'

'And you?'

Foxy smiled. 'Under a beach umbrella, covered in factor fifty. The vampire of St Tropez.' She glanced around her. 'It all seems a long time ago now.'

'Boys?'

'Well . . . there was this one boy.'

'Go on.'

'He was Moroccan, I think, and he sold caramelized peanuts on the beach. He used to stare at me with these sad, golden eyes. We never spoke. It was the perfect relationship.'

'And that was it for the entire summer?'

'Not *quite* . . .'

'Eleanor, Jessica. How nice to have you back!'

Instinctively, the two girls straightened their posture. 'Thank you, Miss Allen,' they replied in unison, as the principal of the Arcadia School of Performing Arts walked past.

'I *never* know what that woman's thinking,' hissed Foxy.

'I think that's what she wants,' said Jess. 'It gives her power over us. But she hasn't totally gone over to the Dark Side.'

'You think not?'

'Well, she could have expelled all four of us last term.'

Foxy looked thoughtful as they continued towards the dormitory block. Neither of them particularly wanted to revisit that day, the previous June, when they and their two room-mates had bunked off school to appear as walk-ons in a feature film. Everything had gone horribly wrong. Alex Karman, the star they'd risked everything to get close to, had turned out to be an arrogant drama queen, and shooting the scene with him had gone on for so long that they'd had to ring the school and ask to be picked up. Unsurprisingly, Miss Allen had not been amused, and they'd been grounded for the rest of term.

'You're right,' said Foxy. 'I guess that could have turned out worse.'

Jess shuddered. Being expelled from Arcadia would have meant the end of everything – her dreams of a career on the stage, on TV and maybe even in films. In the end, though, Miss Allen had been merciful, and the cloud had proved to have a silver lining. Grounded, Jess had spent much of the time working on her acting. She'd understudied the lead in the first-year end-of-term play, and a lucky break had seen her step into the shoes of the scarily beautiful Shannon Matthews. For a single, never-to-be-forgotten performance, she'd played the role of Titania, queen of the fairies, in *A Midsummer Night's Dream*.

As if to greet the two friends, the lights flickered on in their dormitory block. Inside, there was a faint chill and the familiar smell of school. Dragging their cases up the stairs to the first floor, they arrived, panting, at Room 10.

'So, here we are again,' said Jess, throwing open the door.

'Ladies,' said Ash, stepping towards them, arms outstretched. 'Welcome back!'

Ashanti Taylor was still wrapped in her coat and scarf and, as the three of them hugged, Jess felt a tremor run through her.

'Look,' said Ash, holding out a slim hand. 'I'm shivering. Why can't they turn the central heating on? Seriously, girlfriends, I wasn't brought up to live like this.'

Jess laughed. 'Ash, you are such a princess. It's only September.'

'No sign of Spike?' asked Foxy. Verity Nash,

otherwise known as Spike, was the fourth of the room-mates.

'Not yet,' said Ash.

Jess swung her case on to her bed. 'Let's go to the dining hall,' she suggested. 'I'm starving.'

'Already?' Foxy raised an elegantly arched eyebrow. 'Jess, we've only been back here five minutes.'

'That's quite long enough,' said Jess firmly.

2

Five minutes later, they were sitting with steaming cups of tea in front of them. Other Arcadians drifted into the dining hall in small, chattering groups, looking around as they entered, waving, hugging, and searching each others' faces for signs of change.

The hubbub grew. Further up the table, a long-established trio took their places: Shannon Matthews and her sidekicks Kelly Wilkinson and Flick Healey. As usual, all three were dressed to impress in designer-branded hoodies and T-shirts. For much of the previous term Shannon and Jess had got on so badly they'd barely spoken to each other, and it hadn't helped that Shannon had suspected Jess of trying to steal her boyfriend.

Shannon had been wrong; Jess hadn't tried to do anything of the sort. But Johnny Finn was very good-looking and had seemed to like her a lot, and somehow – she really, *really* hadn't planned this – they'd ended up kissing in the boys' locker room. For a split second everything had been wonderful, but only for a split second, because they'd been seen. And shortly afterwards – Jess still froze with horror remembering the scene – she had walked into the dining hall to be met with a chorus of *Bitch, bitch, bitch!* from Shannon and her friends. That had been bad enough, but even worse had been the realization she'd never meant that much to Johnny. All that attention he'd paid her – all those meaningful looks, all those text messages – had just been part of his game. He was a player, and she'd been played.

Well, it wasn't going to happen again, and she and Shannon were now officially quits. They weren't friends exactly, but they had a wary respect for each other, especially since Jess had taken over Shannon's role in the end-of-term play. Now the summer was over and the autumn term was beginning. From today, they were all second years. A chance to start again, surely?

'Hey, Bailey,' said Shannon, fixing Jess with eyes of swimming-pool blue. 'I hear you survived Titania. Hear you were pretty good, in fact. Almost as good as me!'

Jess grinned. 'Well, I remembered the words and managed not to fall flat on my bum –'

7

'I'm sure you'd have bounced back,' smirked Flick.

With an effort, Jess ignored her. When Flick and Kelly were with Shannon, protected by the force field of her glamour, they often liked to have a go at people. Not in a really nasty way, but not in a completely jokey way either. There was usually a little sting in there, somewhere.

Presumably, thought Jess, the pair of them hadn't sussed that she and Shannon had signed a truce. A truce that she wasn't going to endanger by having anything more to do with Johnny. No way in the world.

'That's a gorgeous bracelet, Shannon,' said Ash, and Shannon smiled. From the way that she was showing the bracelet off, turning her wrist so that the stones caught the light, it was obvious that she wanted to be asked about it.

'I know, right? It's crystal. Crystal and silver. I had to wear it for this modelling job, and they let me keep it.'

'That's cool,' said Foxy. 'Have you joined an agency then?'

'I'm with Tempest,' said Shannon. 'They talent-spotted me outside Topshop in London. A lot of the top agencies recruit their models there. They know it's popular, so on Saturday mornings they have people looking out for girls with, like, really good figures and cheekbones and stuff.' She shrugged modestly.

Jess smiled. 'That's me ruled out.'

'That's so not true, Jessica,' said Shannon. 'With help, and some good hair products, you could look . . . y'know. Fine!' She smiled. 'Are you hoping to get into the pantomime?'

Jess had heard about the pantomime, which took place in a local theatre each Christmas. But because she'd only arrived at the school that summer – two terms later than everyone else in her year – she didn't know much about it.

'Er, yes, I guess so,' she said vaguely. 'Are you?'

'Not sure if I'll have time. The way things are going, I'm likely to be too busy with the modelling.'

'So, do you have, like, a portfolio and everything?' Foxy asked.

'Sure,' said Shannon casually, reaching into her bag. 'Take a look.'

The portfolio was a stylish matt grey, with 'TEMPEST Models' imprinted on the cover. Inside were a dozen or so studio photographs. Shannon looking taut and athletic in a Hollister bikini, Shannon moody in skinny jeans and tight white T, Shannon laughing in a Lipsy minidress.

'That's my favourite,' said Flick. It was a swimwear advert from *Mizz* magazine, showing Shannon and a sleepy-eyed boy holding hands

9

on a beach. Shannon was wearing the crystal bracelet.

'You look great,' said Jess. 'And that guy looks nice too.'

'Nice?' said Kelly. 'He's *gorgeous*. I could totally . . . Oh my God.' Her voice flattened. 'Look who's here.'

It was Spike. Seeing her, Jess, Ash and Foxy jumped to their feet, the Tempest portfolio forgotten. Spike was a bit of a legend at Arcadia, not least because of her appearance. Last term she'd had a punky bat-girl crop; now it was a choppy asymmetric cut. Only Spike could have got away with the look. Or, for that matter, the charity-shop sweater and the baggy combat pants.

By the time they'd finished saying their hellos – which Spike, being deaf, answered in sign language – Shannon and the others were making their way out of the dining-hall doors. If they weren't going to be the centre of attention, there was no way they were sticking around.

'God, those girls can be a nightmare,' said Foxy, watching them go.

Spike gave an elegant shrug of her shoulders.

'Whatever.' Ash looked around brightly at the others. 'So. The summer holidays. Who's going first?'

As they talked, Jess looked at her friends. Ash,

with her long-lashed eyes and smooth, dark-cinammon complexion. Despite the fact that she was the youngest of the four room-mates, the Hampshire dentist's daughter was very much the sensible one. The one whose clothes were always put away, whose toothpaste tube always had the top on, whose class timetable was neatly Blu-tacked to the wall by her bed. When they'd been planning the trip to the film set, it had been Ash who sounded the note of caution.

When she let loose her big, rippling voice, though, you saw another side to Ashanti Taylor – a risk-taker, prepared to try anything. Pop, soul, R&B, she took it all in her stride. Jess thought she was awesome, but Ash herself wasn't so sure. 'I'm just another girl who can sing,' she'd told Jess. 'There are thousands of us out there, all wanting the same thing. To make a name, carve out a career, win respect – it's gonna be hard. It's gonna be *really* hard.'

And Foxy. What could you say about Foxy? That mane of red hair. Those cool green eyes and the knowing way that she had about her. Her parents were, as she put it, 'in the business'. Her dad was something in TV and her mum had a casting agency, so Foxy herself had grown up in the showbiz bubble. Jess came from Mitcham in south London, where the high point of the day was a walk to the shops or to feed the ducks on the common, and she had always thought that Foxy's life sounded thrillingly sophisticated, but the other girl had assured her that it wasn't all like that. 'Sure, once in a blue moon you come home and there's some big star sitting at the kitchen table, but mostly it's just deals and contracts and stuff. And it never stops. The phones are never switched off.'

Behind that confident front, Jess realized, her friend was often lonely. 'I mean, last Boxing Day, OK? I came down to breakfast to find a note saying that Mum had flown to LA. And I'm like, hey! We were supposed to go ice-skating. But then I found these guests tickets on her desk to this big charity concert with Jay-Z and everyone, and, I mean, *she* wasn't around, so I rang my friend, and we were in these VIP seats and went to the after-party and it was, you know, great. So . . .'

The home lives of the four of them were very different, Jess had realized, even if they all shared a similar dream. And strangely, although Foxy didn't have a specific talent, she was the one Jess found it easiest to imagine actually living that dream. Whether it was as the face of a new perfume, or fronting some new, must-see TV programme, Foxy was clearly going to be *someone*.

Of all her room-mates, Jess was closest to

Spike. From her first day at Arcadia, she and the willowy Scottish girl had shared an instinctive understanding. Spike's deafness had never been an issue for Jess, and they communicated in a number of ways. Spike was an accomplished lip-reader, which was fine for one-way conversations, but you couldn't have a real friendship if you were doing all the talking; it had to work both ways. So, like Ash and Foxy, Jess had decided to learn sign language. She'd found it really difficult to start with, but she'd stuck with it, and now she was starting to get the hang of it.

Spike was completely fluent, of course, and their exchanges were a bit like predictive texting, with Spike completing words and sentences for Jess with a questioning look as if to say 'Am I right? Is this the word you meant?' And then at other times – at the end of a long school day, perhaps, when Jess was just too tired to concentrate – they'd get out their phones and lie on their beds swapping texts, laughing about the hopelessness of boys and the boringness of geography and the most flattering cut for a leotard, and other vital matters. Spike was very sensitive to other people's moods. She could read Jess at a glance and seemed to know instinctively when to offer sympathy and when to keep her distance. It made her a very special friend.

Spike's summer holidays, in contrast to Foxy's, had been low-key. Her parents owned a cafe in a Highland village, from where, most days, Spike caught the bus into Inverness to take a ballet class at the dance school there. The rest of the day was spent helping her parents in the cafe or hanging out with the friends she'd grown up with.

And then in August, she told the others, she'd been to a summer school run by the Scottish Ballet. To begin with the teachers had been surprised to have a non-hearing girl in their classes, but then they'd seen her dance and everything had been all right. Spike was severely but not totally deaf, so although she couldn't hear music in the usual way, she was able to sense it. As she put it, she could 'hear the vibrations'.

'Any boys there?' Ash asked.

'Yes,' signed Spike. 'But no! How about you?'

'Well . . .' began Ash dramatically, and they all leant in closer. 'We went to Cornwall. And my dad got it into his head that we should all have surfing lessons. And I was like totally no way . . . until I saw the instructor!'

'Fit, by any chance?' inquired Foxy.

'Super-fit, with this streaky blond hair, and super-tanned skin, and eyes that just . . .'

'So what did he actually . . . *teach* you?' asked Jess.

'Well, basically, he'd hold the board, and I'd lie there, holding on tight. And then every so often a wave came along, and I'd fall off and he'd have to rescue me.'

'In his strong, super-tanned arms?'

'That sort of thing.'

'Tragic,' signed Spike, shaking her head.

'You're right,' said Ash regretfully.

'How old was he?' asked Foxy.

'Like . . . eighteen or something.'

'So did you actually learn anything?' asked Spike.

'I learnt that he had a girlfriend called Kerry. She came to help him teach one day, and he put her in charge of me. "This is Ashley," he told her. "See if you can get her standing up." I was soooo vexed – I mean, he couldn't even get my name right, that's how much he'd noticed me – so the next wave that came, I stood up on the board and rode it all the way in. Just to show him.'

'Sounds like he had you pretty well figured out,' said Jess.

Ash rolled her eyes. 'How about you? How was your summer?'

Jess shrugged. 'It was mixed. My dad was home, on his holiday break from Saudi, but he's with this new girlfriend now – I mean, I say girlfriend, she must be at *least* thirty-five – so she was kind of, you know, around the place . . .'

'How was that?' asked Ash.

'Oh ... All right, I guess. She's being very careful not to rush things. Slightly scared of me, I think.'

'I bet she is,' said Foxy. 'If she can't make you like her, she's got problems. And I'm guessing she knows that.'

'Whatever. I just want ... God, I don't know,' said Jess. 'I want things to be how they were before she came along, but I want my dad to be happy too, y'know?'

'So was she around the whole time?'

'No, just for a month or so, and then she had to deal with some family stuff, outside London, so Dad and I went to Suffolk for a fortnight. To the sea.' And that had been lovely. Long walks along the beach, seabirds, fish-and-chip suppers, wrinkling her nose and feeling the sunburn.

'So when did you snog the pet-shop boy?' asked Foxy.

'You *what*?' signed Spike.

'I didn't!' said Jess. 'When we got back to London I worked in this pet shop owned by my Auntie Rena, and there was a boy working there, but nothing happened. Well, not quite nothing. Like Foxy says, he tried to snog me, but I didn't let him.'

Ash rolled her eyes. 'So basically, despite our

beauty, talent and all-round fabulousness, not one of us got any summer loving at all.'

One by one they shook their heads.

'Spike?' said Ash.

Spike looked into the middle distance, the ghost of a smile touching her lips.

Ash folded her arms. 'Verity Nash, you're a sly and wicked woman, and I'm ordering you to tell us exactly what you got up to.'

'Let's just say that . . .' Spike spelt out with calculated slowness, her fingers extended in front of her. 'Texts. Have been. Exchanged.'

'Olly!' whispered Jess.

Spike nodded.

'For the whole summer?' Ash asked.

Spike nodded again.

'Wow!' breathed Jess. 'That's so great!'

'So have you seen him yet?' asked Foxy.

Spike shook her head.

'Ten weeks,' Ash breathed. 'You've been swapping texts for *ten weeks*!'

Jess smiled at Spike. Olly Francis was in their year at Arcadia, and Jess had seen the first signs of his and Spike's romance at the end of the previous term. He was a nice guy – he'd been particularly kind to Jess in the previous term, when she'd been having trouble with her singing – and he was handsome too, with his red-gold hair and fine, sensitive features.

'So what's the last one say?' Ash asked.

Spike handed Jess her phone and they passed it round.

Back 6:00 CWTCUx♥

'*Be back six o'clock. Can't wait to see you. Kiss. Heart,*' translated Ash. 'What's the general opinion, people?'

'Hmm . . . Not bad,' mused Foxy. 'I'd have liked to see another couple of Xs, though. Ideally.'

Ash nodded. 'I agree. One seems a bit, I dunno. It's kind of the minimum. And that single heart symbol. It's like he's playing it safe. It's not like, say, MULU.'

'What's MULU?' asked Jess.

'Miss You, Love You,' said Ash. 'Don't tell me Johnny Finn never sent you that?'

'Never,' said Jess, a trace of regret in her voice.

'Probably couldn't spell it,' said Foxy.

Ash smiled. 'Last term, Zane texted me MULU and signed it LP.'

'Don't tell us,' said Jess.

'Lovesick Puppy!'

'Oh please!' murmured Foxy as Spike mimed sticking her fingers down her throat.

'And is the puppy still lovesick?' enquired Jess.

'We split up for the summer holidays,' admitted Ash.

'That boy's a fool,' signed Spike.

Ash stared at her tea. 'Things haven't been easy for him. At home, I mean. He . . .'

'He what?' asked Foxy.

'Doesn't matter. But I sometimes think just how lucky I've been, growing up with, y'know, so much love and everything. I'm pretty spoilt, really.'

'You're not spoilt,' said Jess. 'And you don't, like, *owe* Zane anything just because you come from a nice family.'

'Jess is right,' signed Spike. 'You can't . . .' She lifted both palms in front of her in a gesture Jess didn't recognize.

Ash shook her head. 'I'm not *sacrificing* myself. I just understand why he's . . .' She looked away. 'Forget it, OK? I did an audition in London last week. Backing singer for a Phoebe Skye charity concert in December. I'm through to the last nine.'

'That's . . . *amazing*!' breathed Jess. 'Why didn't you say?'

'They only want three of us. I don't dare even . . .'

'When's the final audition?'

'They're letting us know.'

'But, Ash,' said Foxy. 'What about the panto?'

'I don't know. I'm not likely to get both – you know what my dancing's like – and if I do I'll just have to see.'

'What exactly happens with the pantomime?' asked Jess. 'I mean, I know that the second years do it each Christmas, but how does the whole thing work?'

'It's at Reading,' said Foxy. 'At the Theatre Royal. The school chooses six boys and six girls. You have to sing and dance, including tap, and do character stuff. Like being sawn in half by the magician, or being the back end of the horse or whatever.'

'Are you going to try for it?'

'Yeah, definitely! And so should you. I was talking to a girl who did it last year – *Aladdin* – and she said it's the *best* fun. You, like, stay at the school in the holidays, but with no rules, and there are loads of parties and stuff . . .'

'It does sound fun . . .' Jess began. And then, catching Spike's eye, fell guiltily silent. No one was ever going to cast a deaf girl in a pantomime chorus.

Spike reached across and squeezed Jess's hand. 'It's fine,' she signed. 'You must go for it. You'd be perfect.'

Jess was about to answer when Foxy leant

urgently forward. 'We have company, people. By the door.'

Jess flicked a glance to her left. It was Olly, moving towards them.

Spike's fingers fluttered. 'Please. *Don't go.*'

'Hey!' Jess called out to the tall half-smiling boy. 'Join us.'

Olly came over. 'So how are you guys?'

He's nervous, thought Jess.

'Oh, y'know, OK,' said Ash.

'Jess, wow, you look . . .'

'Devastatingly attractive?' suggested Jess. 'Fatter?'

'I was going to say thinner, actually.' He looked at Spike. His mouth opened, but no words came out.

'I should unpack,' said Jess. 'Get back to the room.'

'Me too,' said Ash and Foxy together. The three of them stood, picked up their meal trays and moved smartly towards the door. Outside, the light was fading. 'Was that the right thing to do?' murmured Ash. 'Leaving her alone with him like that?'

'She won't thank us,' said Jess. 'But I think it was.'

'Kind of obvious, though, don't you think?'

'Obvious is good,' said Foxy. 'She likes him, he

likes her. He knows we know, she knows he knows we know . . .'

'I just hope he realizes how special she is,' said Jess.

'I'm sure he does,' said Ash. 'But you know what boys are like. They don't have fully functioning brains.'

'You're right,' said Foxy, hunching into her hot-pink coat. 'I can't think why we bother with them.'

3

Lying in bed that night, Jess thought about the summer's end, and about her dad. About the feeling that, for all his efforts to make time for her, he was slipping away.

Her mum had walked out on them a few years earlier, and Jess would never forget the day she came home from an after-school tap class to find the cat mewing for its supper and a note on the kitchen table. Susan Bailey, they discovered, had gone to South Africa with a sports physiotherapist called Derrick.

After she'd left, Jess and her dad had done their best to look after each other. The whole thing had brought them closer. They'd shared so much. And then, at the end of the summer term, he'd showed up with a girlfriend. Perhaps Jess should have known that sooner or later someone else was bound to come along. He was still quite young, after all. For a dad.

Jess hadn't seen her mum since she'd left them. There had been texts and emails promising that she was making arrangements to fly up from South Africa, where she lived with Creepy Eyebrows (as Jess had renamed Derrick), but somehow these trips never quite worked out. A recent email, though, had worried Jess.

I hear there's someone new in your father's life. I hope she's not taking advantage of him. He was always SUCH a soft touch. Perhaps I'll come and check her out!!!

Something about these words had panicked Jess. She hadn't mentioned the email to her dad because she'd been pretty sure it would upset him. If her mum reappeared now, she didn't know how she'd feel. Angry, she guessed, although deep down, and despite everything that had happened, she still loved her.

Outside in the school grounds, the wind sighed in the trees, infinitely sad, and Jess rolled herself tighter into her duvet. Through the gap in the curtains she could see the night sky and a single faint twinkle. *That's me*, she thought. *A lone star.*

On her bedside locker, her phone vibrated. It was a text from Spike, on the other side of the room. She'd come in quite late, when they'd all been preparing for bed, and hadn't seemed very communicative.

U wake jess?

Yup am now! How dit go w O?

Not gr8 didnt want 2 kiss me
☹!!

Xactly!

Did u talk??

No dumass im def lol :/

Lol ok did O talk?

Nuthin BUT talk

What abt all those lovey txts? xx

Think preferd idea of luv 2 me!!!

Just shy??

Hope so ;)

Boys omg :(

U said it babes

Well, gnight x

Yup c u tomoz x

4

'I am soooo sore,' wailed Jess as she and Kelly Wilkinson pulled on their track tops after ballet class the next morning. 'My feet! God, I hate pointe work. I felt like a hippo doing those *grands jetés*.'

'Didn't you take any classes during the summer?' asked Kelly, undoing her ponytail and shaking out her honey-blonde hair. Annoyingly, Kelly always managed to stay neat and trim on these occasions. She looked fantastic in the silver-grey school-issue leotard and tights, whereas Jess, with her sweat-shiny face and scruffy mouse-brown bun, felt a mess.

'It wasn't always possible,' Jess said.

In fact Jess had done classes off and on throughout the holidays. Ballet, tap, jazz dance and singing. And when she could manage it she'd continued with her online sign-language course too. But the time she'd had with her dad at the beginning of the summer had been so precious. She hadn't wanted to spend half of every day taking long bus rides up to central London and back. Nor did she feel that she could ask him for the cost of the classes, so it was only when she'd worked at the pet shop that she started taking them regularly again.

As it happened, it had all worked out quite well. The evening dance classes, especially, were quite fun affairs. A mixture of students like herself and professionals who wanted a workout before going on stage in the West End. There had been another Arcadia student there, a girl in Jess's year called Georgie Maxwell, who was one of a trio of ballet fanatics nicknamed the Bunheads.

Georgie was rumoured to have very posh parents, and according to Foxy, who always seemed to know about such things, her mum was called the Honourable Pamela Maxwell. Curious to find out if all this was true, Jess had examined Georgie closely for signs of difference – things that would mark her out as being upper class. Disappointingly, though, she looked quite normal, in a Bunhead-ish sort of way, although her hair seemed expensively cut and she had a smoky-pink cashmere cardigan that she'd stuff into her ballet bag as if it was an old T-shirt. And then one day Jess had asked her where exactly she lived and Georgie had answered, slightly unwillingly, that her parents spent most of the time in Wiltshire but also had 'a place sort of behind Harrods' where they stayed when they were in London.

Jess had been to Harrods with her dad. The two of them had wandered around the huge department store for hours, marvelling at the luxury goods and the off-the-scale prices. To have a place 'sort of behind' Harrods meant that the Maxwells must be very rich indeed. To say that you were staying 'sort of above Paws 'n' Claws in the Croydon Road' didn't quite have the same ring to it.

'You know why I love ballet so much?' Georgie said to Jess. 'Because it doesn't matter who you are; you can either get out there and do it, or you can't. In my parents' world, success is all about who you know. If you're not part of that super-rich banker gang, forget it. I mean, my best friends at school – Poppy Rattigan and Paige Purkiss . . . Poppy's parents are basically hippies, living in Devon, and Paige's dad works in a garage in Romford, in Essex. And the three of us have exactly the same dream: to get into a ballet company. But can I take them home to stay? No *way*. My parents just aren't *formatted* to deal with normal people. They'd be so patronizing I get toe cramps just thinking about it.'

Talking to Georgie, Jess realized that to get the most out of Arcadia and make a future for yourself you had to leave the past and your childhood behind. You had to reinvent yourself: to be the person you wanted to be, not the person everyone thought you were.

After the evening classes, Georgie and Jess would go to a steamy Italian cafe near Leicester Square that was known as a hang-out for actors and dancers. It had felt good to be part of the crowd, listening to talk of agents and auditions, and sharing the backstage gossip over cups of tea – which famous actor was carrying on with which chorus dancer and which reality-show star had fallen flat on her bum on stage the night before. Listening wide-eyed, and hoping that her clothes didn't smell too strongly of the pet shop, Jess had been amazed at some of the stories.

Poor Desmond, the boy who'd tried to kiss her. She'd seen him watching her over the tanks of Fantail goldfish and the sacks of Winalot and Puppy Diet. Jess had always treated him as a friend and didn't think she'd done anything to suggest otherwise. But on her last afternoon he'd lunged at her when they were out by the bins at the back of the shop, emptying the used shavings from the hamster cages.

Disappointed that she didn't respond, he'd

asked if things might have been different if he'd chosen somewhere more romantic, and she'd told him gently that they wouldn't.

'So what do you think?' asked Kelly.

Jess came to with a start. 'Sorry, I was miles away. What do I think about what?'

'About modelling.'

'You modelling, you mean?'

'Of course me, durr!'

'Um, yeah!' Jess blinked. 'Go for it! I mean, you're really pretty, and you've got the hair and the figure and stuff.'

'You think?' murmured Kelly pensively, angling her body to see herself in the dance-studio mirror.

'I think. But ask Shannon, she seems to be the expert.'

Kelly rolled her eyes. 'And doesn't she just let us know it.'

In the mirror, Jess could see Foxy undoing her bun. Beside her, Spike was wrapping the ribbons round her pointe shoes, waiting for Kelly to leave. Spike and Kelly had never got on. Kelly was a good dancer, the kind that teachers always made a fuss of, and Jess guessed that she had rows of ballet-exam rosettes pinned up at home. Unfortunately for Kelly – and this must have been seriously annoying for her – she'd arrived at Arcadia in the same term as one of the most talented dancers in the school's history. Dancing was Spike's voice, her song; it came as naturally to her as breathing, and when she was in class everyone else just faded into the background.

Kelly had never accepted this. She resented Spike, and an incident the previous term had made things worse. With Spike and her room-mates grounded for bunking off to visit a film set, Kelly had taken over the lead dancing role in the end-of-term play. But the ballet sequences had proved too difficult for her and Spike had been reinstated, with Kelly sent back to the chorus.

It hadn't been Spike's fault, but Kelly had blamed her anyway. It had occurred to Jess at the time that Miss Pearl, who was head of dance, might simply have made the steps easier, but this was not the Arcadia way. As far as the school was concerned, you could either do the part or you couldn't. It was tough, but so was the world that the school was preparing them for.

'Whassup?' signed Spike, as Kelly disappeared along the corridor towards the showers.

'She asked me if she should go in for modelling,' said Jess.

'Hope you told her no.'

'Why? She's really nice-looking. And Shannon's doing it.'

'Shannon's got the nose. First thing they check

out at an agency. Kelly has a nose like a banana. They won't take her.'

'How do you know these things?' asked Jess.

'TV. Haven't you seen *Strictly Catwalk*?'

Jess wandered over to the studio mirror. No one, it was safe to say, would be likely to offer her modelling work. Pale and freckly, with eyes the colour of pondwater and hair that went mad if a brush came near it, she was about as far from the catwalk ideal as it was possible to be. 'My nose is just a blob,' she said ruefully. 'And my ears! Total chimpanzee.'

'People love chimpanzees,' said Foxy, zipping up her track top. 'It's that whole practically human thing. And you'll miss drama if you don't get a move on. It's with that new guy, Mr Casey.'

Jess tore herself away from her reflection, and a couple of minutes later, muscles aching, hurried into the crowded theatre studio, where Mr Casey, a floppy-haired type in his mid-twenties, was taking names. Jess barely registered him because there, over by the window, was Johnny Finn. And, seeing those ice-blue eyes, Jess's heart flipped. For all her determination that nothing would happen between them, Johnny had a way of making her feel light-headed and reckless, as if life were a wild adventure starring just the two of them. It faded, that feeling – faded pretty fast, in fact. But it was thrilling while it lasted.

And acting with him, as Titania to his Oberon, had been most thrilling of all. For that brief hour and a half, Jess had let her imagination fly free. She'd never had a boyfriend, not a proper one, but on the outdoor stage that scented summer night she and Johnny had been a couple. And what a couple. Oberon was jealous and scheming, almost evil at times, a real creature of darkness, and Titania was his wilful, spoilt fairy queen. The whole experience had unrolled like a dream and, when Jess thought back to it, she could remember very few of the details. But she could remember the feeling – that terrifying, free-falling moment when she'd first stepped on stage, then the confidence kicking in as everything slowed to an absolute clarity.

She smiled, remembering. In the shabby drama studio, with the rain streaming down the windows, it was as if it had all happened in another life. She was still smiling when Johnny caught her eye and, infuriatingly, she felt herself blushing. With a huge effort, she forced herself to concentrate. Mr Casey was dividing the students into pairs for improvisation exercises. Jess found improv difficult but fun. The idea was that you had to play a part without any preparation at all, making it up as you went along.

'The scene that we're going to improvise is simple,' Mr Casey told them. 'A store detective is accusing a customer of shoplifting. And each pair is going to play the scene in a different way. Everybody up for it?'

They nodded.

'You two first,' said Mr Casey, pointing at Foxy and Zane Johnson, Ash's on–off boyfriend. 'Go for it.'

Pushing his blond hair out of his eyes, Zane placed a hand on Foxy's shoulder. 'Madam,' he began. 'Could I ask you to come with me?'

Foxy turned. 'Might I ask why?'

'I think you know why, madam.'

'Excuse me!' said Foxy. 'I most certainly do not.'

'It's to do with the frozen turkey that is stuffed under your top, ma'am.'

'Turkey?' breathed Foxy. 'How dare you? I am with child!'

Zane sniggered, but recovered himself. 'Never seen a child that shape, ma'am.'

'That's because it is no ordinary child. It is The One. And now I believe I'm going into labour. Please fetch boiling water, surgical instruments and cake.'

By now Zane was laughing so much he couldn't

answer. Foxy curtseyed and then, turning to Mr Casey, flicked him a long, cool green-eyed stare. Jess watched, amazed. Was she *flirting* with him? Did she totally have no brain?

'Well, that was . . . interesting,' said Mr Casey, as the class applauded. Several other pairs replayed the scene in different ways – as musical comedy, Shakespearean tragedy, a cowboy film – and then Mr Casey pointed at Jess and the boy she'd been partnered with, Calvin Okenwe.

'OK, you two. Let's have it as a rom-com. Jessica, you're the store detective.'

Oh no, thought Jess. *Johnny's still watching. Don't look at him! Don't look!*

She looked, of course. And Johnny stared straight back, that knowing half-smile still in place. *Relax*, she told herself, and the words of Colette Jones, Arcadia's head of drama, came back to her. *Use it. Whatever you're feeling, use it.*

She stepped in front of Calvin, allowing her eyes to widen. 'Excuse me, sir,' she whispered. 'Could I ask you to . . . step into the office?'

'Er, why?' He stared at her as if struck by lightning.

'If we could just step into the office, sir, I'll explain.'

Calvin kept his eyes on hers. 'Sure . . . but wait a minute, didn't I see you on the number thirty-one bus this morning? You were wearing a pale blue coat? The colour of your eyes.'

'Please, sir, empty your pockets for me?'

'Of course, if that's what you . . . but . . . what *is* all this stuff? I didn't put it there. I don't even like tinned peaches. Or sardines.'

'Really? That's very strange because neither do I.'

Calvin smiled. 'You were on that bus, weren't you?'

'Well . . .' She smiled faintly. 'Let's just say that I do have a pale blue coat.'

'And a boyfriend?'

'He died in a tragic shelf-stacking accident yesterday afternoon.'

'Then . . . you'll have dinner with me?'

'Oh *yes*!' Jess gasped.

More applause from the class. Jess flashed Johnny a quick glance. He looked kind of impressed, she thought.

'Fast thinking, you two, good effort,' said Mr Casey, running a hand through his floppy fringe. 'Next pair, please.'

'That went well,' whispered Calvin, when they'd taken their places at the back of the class. 'I saw you in *Midsummer Night's Dream* at the end of last term, by the way. You were great!'

'Thanks,' Jess murmured absently.

'So *do* you have a boyfriend?'

She turned to him, surprised.

'Well, do you?'

'Umm . . . could we pay attention there at the back?' said Mr Casey, peering over the heads of the other students. 'Yes, I'm talking to you, Jessica.'

'Sorry,' she mumbled. *This certainly isn't going to help me get into the pantomime.*

Calvin stood up. 'It wasn't her fault, Mr Casey. It was me. I was saying how great she acted.'

A snigger rippled through the class. 'Well, that's very chivalrous, Calvin, but let's leave it till after class, OK? And it's how *well* Jessica acted, not how *great*.'

Calvin grinned. 'Well, I thought she was great!'

Jess shut her eyes and shook her head. When she opened them again Johnny was looking straight at her. He grinned and rolled his eyes sympathetically. Giving in, she grinned back at him.

So, she thought. *No change there then. Johnny's still playing the same old game. And he still belongs to Shannon. Gorgeous, catwalk-perfect Shannon. Nice one, Jess.*

5

'Well, I kind of enjoyed that,' said Foxy, catching up with Jess as they left the classroom. 'And you obviously made a big impression on Calvin.'

'Yeah, right. And made a complete twit of myself at the same time. But what was all that flirty, look-at-me stuff with Mr Casey? Are you, like, insane?'

'He's amazing!'

'Fox, he's a teacher. And you're fourteen.'

'I can dream, can't I?'

'Of what?'

'Oh . . .' Her face took on a faraway look. 'Y'know. Things. Like the dorm block being on fire and him rescuing me.'

Jess shook her head. 'Foxy, squirrels have eaten your brain.'

'Maybe, but the real reason you're cranky is because of Johnny. Admit.'

'OK, a bit. But even so . . .'

Her voice tailed off. Head lowered, clearly upset, a female student was making her way up the corridor from the dance studios. Intercepting her, Jess and Foxy peered through the dishevelled fringe at the mascara-streaked features.

'Flick!' said Foxy. 'What's the matter?'

'My money,' said Flick Healey, her voice trembling. 'Someone in Miss Pearl's class just stole my money.'

Jess looked at Foxy and then back at Flick. 'Are you sure?'

''Course I'm sure,' whispered Flick. 'I zipped it up in my tracksuit pocket and put it on the chair – you know, the one by the piano – and then at the end of the class it wasn't there.'

'The tracksuit?' asked Foxy.

'No, the *money*,' wailed Flick. 'Someone had taken it. Unzipped the pocket and . . .'

'How much?' asked Jess.

'Fifty pounds. A note.'

Jess's eyes widened. She wasn't sure whether she'd ever seen a fifty-pound note. Certainly no one had ever paid for anything with one in the pet shop.

'It was a birthday present from my dad. I literally just got it this morning. God . . . what am I gonna do?'

Jess and Foxy looked at each other. 'You're

really sure you haven't just, like, lost it?' asked Foxy.

Flick looked at her icily. 'Yes, I am sure I haven't just, like, *lost it*.'

'Well, you'd better see Miss Allen then.'

'I guess. Oh my *God*.'

They watched her go. 'Fifty pounds,' murmured Jess. 'Why would you take a fifty-pound note into a ballet class?'

Foxy shrugged. 'Probably meant to take it up to her room later. But I'm glad I'm not in that class. There'll be real trouble if that money doesn't turn up.'

'Ash is in that class,' said Jess.

'You're right. We should warn her.'

Jess nodded. 'Let's just pray the money's found. That it fell out of Flick's pocket or something. Someone might've, you know, seen it on the floor and picked it up, meaning to hand it in.'

The two girls looked at each other. Jess could tell Foxy was thinking the same thing that she was. That while most Arcadia students would have handed the money in to a teacher without a second thought, not all would.

At that moment Calvin swung round the corner. Something about the forced casualness of his walk suggested to Jess that his arrival was no accident.

'Hey, Jess!'

'Calvin.'

He stood there, shuffled a bit and ran a nervous hand through his hair. 'I just wanted to, like, say sorry for getting you into trouble with Mr Casey?'

'No prob.'

'So . . . yeah. I was wondering if you'd fancy, like, coming for a coffee?'

'Er . . .' She glanced at Foxy and then back at Calvin. 'Not right now, if that's OK.' She smiled. 'But thanks for asking.'

'I might just go on asking.'

'Please . . . let's just go on as friends, yeah?'

Calvin nodded. 'You're really stuck on Johnny Finn, aren't you? Well, you know what? You're an idiot. And not half as great-looking as you think you are either.'

Jess turned away, as shocked as if she'd been slapped. When she looked up he was walking away and Foxy was staring after him.

'That is so . . . *unfair*,' Jess gasped. 'What did I . . .?'

'Nothing,' murmured Foxy. 'Nothing at all. God, this place.'

'But I *don't* think I'm great-looking.'

'I know you don't,' said Foxy affectionately, slipping an arm round her shoulders. 'That's what drives them so nuts.'

6

As September became October the first winds came, whirling the leaves from the oaks and beeches that surrounded the Arcadia grounds. Inside the school buildings, clanking sounds from the pipes and radiators announced that the central heating had finally been turned on.

Jess had always loved autumn. At home, in south London, it had meant shining pavements, streetlights flickering on at teatime, and fish-and-chip meals in front of the TV. Here, at Arcadia, the season was more mysterious. Iron-grey skies, the smell of bonfires, and at night the long sigh of the wind. Sometimes, lying in her bed with the darkness pressing at the window, Jess imagined that she and her friends were on a ship, far out at sea. Where were they going? she wondered. Would they ever arrive? Often it seemed as if she drifted for hours on the tide between wakefulness and sleep, between imagining and dreaming.

And then, suddenly, the tinny bell of the alarm clock would drill into their heads until Foxy, groaning, stretched out and slapped it into silence. Ash was always up first, shuffling to the bathroom in her pink velour dressing gown. Then Jess would reach out and shake Spike, who would immediately bury her head beneath the pillow. And another day would begin.

At Arcadia, Jess discovered, it was better not to think too far ahead. So when she got up on a weekday morning she didn't worry about the day's acting, singing and dancing classes, but just looked forward to breakfast. To the short walk from the dorm block to the steamy warmth of the dining hall, and to the cornflakes, toast and tea that were waiting there.

Every day started with ballet class. Comparatively few Arcadians actually went on to become professional ballet dancers, but Miss Allen believed that the ritual and the discipline of classical dance gave her students something special. It taught them how to walk on to a stage and, without speaking a word, command an audience's attention. Arcadians, Miss Allen liked to say, had *presence*.

Ballet class was also a reality check. That studio mirror reminded the students, day after day, who they really were. And, as Jess was discovering, it was only when you knew who you really were that you could set about the business of becoming someone else. It wasn't so easy, looking yourself in the eye like that – realizing that your nose was a blob, your ears looked like a monkey's . . . But you had to accept yourself. You had to say: *OK! For better or for worse, this is what I have to work with.* And somehow, Jess found, this set her free. Free to transform herself into someone people found beautiful or funny or tragic or whatever, even though the original Jessica Bailey wasn't any of those things. At least, she didn't think she was.

It was very personal, this transformation thing, and Jess didn't like to talk about it, or even think too hard about it, in case she spooked the process. The others, she knew, didn't see performing in the same way. Foxy, for example, wasn't really interested in becoming anyone else. What she wanted was to become a smarter, funnier, shinier version of herself. Spike never really stopped being herself either, but there was something so mysterious and other-worldly about Spike that she didn't need to. And then there was Ash, who seemed to be two completely different people – the super-cautious dentist's daughter from Basingstoke, and the girl with the smoky-gold voice who, when she sang, dared everything.

After a painfully self-conscious first term, Jess

was beginning to enjoy her own singing. Shortly after she'd arrived at Arcadia, Olly had appointed himself her unofficial voice coach. Her problem, he'd discovered, was more to do with lack of confidence than lack of voice. She could sing well enough, but found it difficult to be expressive in front of her classmates.

So they'd taken to walking in the school grounds after singing classes and, with her voice fully warmed up, Jess would go over the numbers they'd worked on in class. Somehow, with Olly, it didn't matter if she made a fool of herself. And gradually, as the weeks had passed, she'd come to realize that she wasn't so bad after all. Compared to, say, Georgie Maxwell or Poppy Rattigan, who really *couldn't* sing (not that they cared), she was an operatic genius. Mr Huntley had noticed the change. Noticed that Jess opened her shoulders and smiled when she sang, rather than hunching up and frowning apologetically. And that despite her initial shyness she actually had a nice, useful, mezzo-soprano voice.

But was it good enough for the chorus of *Cinderella*? On the Wednesday evening following the turning-on of the central heating, Jess caught up with Olly as he left the main building after tea.

'I want you to teach me a song,' she told him. 'Something to really blow Mr Huntley away.'

'This wouldn't have anything to do with the pantomime, would it?'

Jess smiled. 'Maybe.'

It was only a week now until the names of the chosen second years went up on the school notice board. The panto was famously exhausting, with six matinees and six evening performances a week, and if you were in it you couldn't go home for Christmas. But that didn't stop almost everyone in the year from wanting to be chosen, or from trying their hardest to impress the teachers who would be choosing. Panto-fever was in the air, and Jess was as caught up in the excitement of it all as everyone else.

Olly nodded, and they walked for a moment in silence, their breath rising in misty puffs in front of them. 'How about "I Dreamed a Dream" from *Les Miz*?' he suggested. 'That's a show-stopper. And it's easily within your range. If we work on it over the weekend, you could do it in Mr Huntley's class on Monday.'

'That would be good timing,' Jess agreed.

'In that case, let's find a music room right now.' He glanced at his watch. 'I can give you an hour, then I've got a date with Audrey.'

'Audrey?'

'Audrey Hepburn. The sixties actress. One of

the guys on my corridor's downloaded *Breakfast at Tiffany's*.'

'OK. Sure you've got time?'

'For you? Always.'

'Olly, you're a brilliant friend. Seriously.'

'I know. So be brilliant too.'

A few minutes later they were in a dusty cupboard-like room on the first floor of the main building. The room contained an elderly upright piano, a single wobbly chair and a stack of music scores. From the ballet studio next door came the faint thump of boys practising jumps.

'Do you know how to play this?' Jess asked.

Olly smiled. 'Just about,' he said, pulling the *Les Misérables* songbook from the stack of scores.

'I Dreamed a Dream' was a good choice. Olly, inevitably, proved to be a highly capable pianist, and by the time that he closed the songbook forty minutes later Jess had a pretty good idea of how she'd perform it. Another couple of practice sessions and it would be ready for Mr Huntley.

'Thank you,' said Jess sincerely as they descended the stairs.

'Likewise, babes. I'll text you about meeting up over the weekend.'

'OK. Enjoy the film.'

'I will. It's so romantic . . . That bit with the cat – I *always* cry. And Audrey's clothes!'

Jess was tempted to remind Olly that there was a real, living and very romantically inclined girl just longing for him to call her, but it didn't quite seem the moment. And so, a little guiltily, she said nothing.

7

On Wednesday morning, shortly after breakfast, Miss Allen walked from her office to the school notice board, an A4 sheet of paper in her hand. As she approached, her heels clicking briskly on the parquet floor, a crowd of expectant second years parted to let her through. From their position on the outskirts of the group, Jess and her room-mates watched as the head teacher pinned the notice to the board. The casting for the pantomime. As a non-singer, Spike knew there was no chance of her being chosen, but she had come to lend support and dispense hugs of congratulation or sympathy as necessary. Standing next to her, Jess could hear the *tick-tick-tick* of her earphones. Shakira, it sounded like.

Jess had mixed feelings about the panto. She wanted, very badly, to be chosen – to know that, as far as the school was concerned, she was on course. And it would be amazing fun. There

49

would be the thrill of rehearsals and performances, and on top of that the strange, exciting business of staying at the school in the holidays, being allowed to come and go as they pleased, to wear what they liked and generally live without rules. And it would be Christmas! How could it all not be magic?

And she stood a good chance, especially after Monday's singing class, when she'd stood up and sung 'I Dreamed a Dream', winning a thoughtful 'Not bad, Jessica, not bad at all!' from Mr Huntley. But if she was chosen it would mean seeing very little of her dad, and missing out on the things they always did together at this time of year. Jess had a particular memory from the year before of the two of them emerging from the Underground at Oxford Circus, in London, on Christmas Eve. Everyone was doing their last-minute present shopping, and on the Tube train it had been standing room only. Jess and her dad been swept up the wet station steps to join a sea of people on the street. It was mid-afternoon, the light was fading and a soft drizzle falling. And then, as if by magic, the Christmas lights burst into life. High above their heads, giant gold nets hung like jewelled cobwebs between the great department stores. Above Oxford Street, as far as the eye could see, were diamond-white starbursts, ice-blue snowflake crystals, and cascades of sugar-pink and lime. Above the glittering river of Regent Street, neon Simbas and Bambis were frozen mid-leap. It was as if the whole spectacle had been arranged just for them. Jess couldn't remember clearly how the afternoon had ended – shopping, tea in a cafe, the Tube home – but that first moment was etched on her mind. It represented everything that she knew, deep down, was slipping away: her childhood, and the time when she had her dad to herself.

In its place, exciting and terrifying, was the future, a realm in which she had to create her own magic. Really, Jess knew, there was no choice to be made. For better or worse, she had to let go, to leave the past behind her. And, as Miss Allen turned away from the board and marched smartly back towards her office, Jess swept forward with the rest.

Cast for Cinderella, she read. *Theatre Royal, Reading, December fifteenth to January fifth.*

She was in! There was her name – 'Yaaayy!' – and there was Foxy's too. And Johnny's! Finally they'd be performing in a real theatre, in front of a paying audience. Jess scanned the other names – *Kelly, Flick, Emilia, Emma* – and felt a stab of shame at her triumphant outburst. Ash's name wasn't on the list.

'Really, I don't mind,' said Ash, forcing a grin. 'I'm probably the world's worst tap dancer. And if I get the Phoebe Skye gig . . .'

'You'll get it,' said Foxy firmly. 'You'll totally get it.'

More surprising was the fact that Shannon wasn't chosen. But over the next couple of days Shannon put the word around that she'd asked Miss Allen not to be included, because it would interfere with her modelling work. And where Shannon went it seemed that Johnny followed. To begin with he was at the top of the list of boys chosen, but by the next morning his name had been crossed out and replaced with Calvin's. Jess was surprised and secretly disappointed at this, but Foxy soon put her straight. 'You don't really think that Shannon's going to let Johnny do the panto with you, do you? All those late nights and cast parties? In your dreams, girl! She's not that stupid.'

'I don't think I'm much of a threat to her,' Jess protested.

'It's not you she distrusts, it's him,' said Foxy. 'Everybody knows that he fancies you. And the two of you do have, y'know, a bit of a history . . .'

'Wouldn't happen again, Fox. Really.'

'Well, there's always Calvin.'

'Oh please. Calvin hates me.'

'Sure he does,' said Foxy. 'One smile from you and he'd melt like cookie-dough ice cream.'

Jess shook her head. Love, for the Room 10 girls, was turning into a bit of a disaster area. Jess was trying to forget Johnny, and failing miserably; Zane showed no sign of wanting to get back with Ash; and Spike and Olly didn't seem to be going anywhere either.

Foxy, usually so cool and self-possessed, was coming up with ever more nutty romantic scenarios involving Mr Casey. These all started differently – usually with some terrifying natural catastrophe – but all ended the same way, with Foxy being carried to safety in the drama teacher's arms.

'To be honest, I think it's unlikely that the school would be hit by an avalanche,' said Ash, who unlike the others, took her geography lessons seriously. 'You might fall into an oxbow lake, though.'

'Oxbow lakes don't really do it for me,' said Foxy, rolling her green eyes at the ceiling. 'Honestly, you people with your teenage crushes . . . You can't *begin* to understand the pain of true love.'

8

Two days after the *Cinderella* cast list went up, Spike was called to the school office, where she was told by Miss Allen that the school had put her up for an audition in London. It was for a role in *The Nutcracker*, which the English National Ballet would be performing that Christmas at the Royal Albert Hall. The auditions were to be held a fortnight later, at the company's headquarters in Kensington. The Bunheads – Poppy, Paige and Georgie – would also be going.

As soon as Spike had told them the news, her three room-mates went to ask Miss Allen if they could go to London with her, to provide encouragement and support.

The school principal looked at them thoughtfully. 'Well,' she said, 'I think it's probably time to draw a line under last term's exploit. Speak to Miss Pearl; there should be room in the van. You might not be allowed into the actual audition, though. That's by invitation only.'

'Do you think our girls have a chance?' Ash asked.

'We wouldn't have put them forward if we didn't,' said Miss Allen.

'That would be so cool: Arcadia students dancing with the English National Ballet,' mused Foxy.

'Well, let's keep our fingers crossed. And now, if you girls would excuse me . . .'

Chorusing their thanks, the three of them ran outside.

'Yay!' whooped Foxy. 'London shopping!'

'Quarter pounder and large fries,' breathed Jess. 'I'm desperate for some proper food.'

'And when are we going to do all this shopping and eating, exactly?' asked Ash. 'We'll probably have to wait in the van while Spike and the Bunheads do their stuff, and then be driven straight back.'

'Oh boo,' said Foxy. 'We'll find a way. Like we will when you go up for your Phoebe Skye audition.'

Walking back to their room, the three stopped at the entrance to the main building to check the notice board for any lesson changes or announcements. A small cutting announced that a former Arcadian had been accepted by the Royal Shakespeare Company for a production of *Love's Labours Lost*, and there was a note from Miss Sim about the new discount range of boys' tap shoes at the school shop. *Make sure they are a good fit, especially round the heels*, Miss Sim advised, with much underlining. *Blisters are not an acceptable reason for missing class.*

It was a printed announcement on headed school writing paper, however, that the three girls stopped to stare at, even though they'd all read it before.

A student has reported the loss of a fifty-pound note. If anyone has found it, or knows anything about its disappearance, it is essential that they speak to myself or to a member of staff. All information will be held in the strictest confidence.
    Wanda Allen – Head Teacher.

'Obviously no one's come forward,' murmured Ash grimly.

'I still think Flick might have just lost it,' said Foxy. 'I wouldn't put it past her, she's pretty scatty.'

'Someone would have found it by now, surely,' protested Jess.

'Not if it's at the bottom of one of her drawers,

mixed up with tights and socks and old Snickers wrappers. I went in that room once, the one she shares with Kelly and Shannon, and her area was a tip. And my standards are not high, as you know.'

Jess smiled. 'So what do you think'll happen?'

Foxy shrugged. 'My guess is that Miss Allen knows that Flick's a bit of a ditz. So nothing, basically. But if anything else goes missing there'll be big trouble!'

When they got back to the room, Jess decided to work on her signing. Apart from helping her to communicate with Spike, it was a useful skill to have for the future. As an actress, Jess knew, she was entering the most competitive profession of all. Part of her didn't want to think about this. Of *course* she was going to be one of the successful ones. One of the few who worked all the time, moving easily between theatre and film and TV, and hearing the whispers of recognition wherever she went.

But part of her was coldly realistic. At any given time, she knew – and this was a statistic that Arcadia hammered into them – over ninety per cent of actors were likely to be out of work. And that ninety per cent included the best of them. It wasn't a possibility that she'd face periods of unemployment; it was a cast-iron certainty. Actors called it 'resting', and many of them 'rested' for months or even years at a time. So if she didn't want to spend half her life on unemployment benefit, or cleaning out hamster cages for Auntie Rena, it was worth learning something else as a backup. And fate seemed to have thrown sign language her way. The online course was tough, but Jess made herself do a little each day.

When Spike returned to the room, Jess flipped her laptop shut. Her friend, it turned out, was still on a nervous high about the audition.

'You'll be fine,' Jess signed carefully. 'When they see you, they'll want you.'

Spike wasn't so sure. 'There'll be girls from Elmhurst, Central, Tring, the Royal . . .' she replied, fingerspelling the famous school names. 'The best of the best.'

'You're the best of the best,' said Ash loyally, throwing open a window to air the room, as she insisted on doing every day, to the groans of the others.

'I'm weird-looking and I'm deaf.'

'That's true,' said Foxy. 'But think of the publicity. *Weird-looking deaf girl to dance with the English National Ballet* . . . I can see it now.'

Her eyes narrowing, Spike reached into her bag, took out a pointe shoe and threw it at Foxy, who ducked. Ribbons trailing, the shoe sailed out of the window. A moment later there was an unmistakably adult yelp.

All four girls hit the floor, Foxy giggling uncontrollably.

'Who was that?' whispered Ash.

Jess raised herself inch by inch, until the corner of the window was level with her eye. Outside, on the gravel path, two women were looking up at her. 'Oh my God,' she hissed. 'It's Colette and La Perla.'

Colette Jones was head of drama, Serena Pearl head of dance. Their expressions suggested that, in general, they weren't keen on having manky old pointe shoes thrown at them.

Spike winced at the others. *Sorry*, she mouthed.

Foxy, who by now had tears of laughter running down her face, could only shake her head, and this set Jess and Spike off too.

'It's not *funny*,' hissed Ash, but this only made them worse.

Finally Jess stood up. 'I'll go down,' she said, wiping her eyes.

Spike followed her. Not daring to look at each other in case they cracked up again, they presented themselves to the two teachers. Miss Pearl was holding the pointe shoe.

'Jessica Bailey,' said Colette Jones resignedly. 'Now tell me, how did I just *know* you'd be involved?'

'Sorry, Miss Jones,' said Jess. 'It was an accident. The, um, window was open, and . . .'

'Yes, I think we can more or less piece the story together,' said Miss Pearl, handing the pointe shoe back to Spike.

'Tell her sorry,' Spike signed, biting back a snigger.

'She apologizes,' said Jess. 'It won't happen again.'

Miss Pearl gave them a wintry smile. 'Don't worry, the injury wasn't fatal. But, Verity dear, could you at least try to keep out of trouble until after this weekend?' She turned to Colette Jones. 'Verity is auditioning for a role in the English National Ballet's *Nutcracker*. I have high hopes for her.'

Colette nodded. 'Excellent. And, Jessica, you might consider keeping your nose clean too. You never know what might be coming up.'

9

Singing class again, and Mr Huntley had asked the girls to prepare 'Good Morning Baltimore' from *Hairspray*. Jess had worked hard at it, but she still wasn't confident that she could get through it note-perfectly. She could do the belting bits, but there was a key change on a long note that tripped her up almost every time, even when she was alone in Room 10, singing to Ash's velvet rabbit, Shasha.

'Just go for it,' Olly whispered to her as they took their places. 'Sing to me, if you like.'

'OK, as long as you're nowhere near Johnny.'

'Jess, you *have* to get over that boy.'

'I know, I'm trying. But . . .'

Olly squeezed her wrist. 'Like I said, sing to *me*, yeah? Ignore him. Totally.'

'I'll totally try.'

In the event the class didn't go too badly. The boys had started, singing 'The Nicest Kids in

Town', also from *Hairspray*, while the girls filled in the *bop-bee-bas* and *sha-na-nas* in the background. Johnny, typically, gave a magnetic, look-at-me performance, jiving and twisting as he sang, and watching him Jess sighed. Showing off was as natural to Johnny as breathing. It never seemed to occur to him that he looked anything other than fabulous – which of course was why he and Shannon had hooked up. So that the two of them could live in a little bubble of round-the-clock fabulousness, adored by a chorus of the shiny-nosed, the mousy-haired and the generally unglamorous.

'I sort of got it,' Jess said to Olly after the class. 'That key change, I mean.'

'Well, you sort of didn't too,' Olly replied as they crossed the lawn in front of the main building. 'You need to take a bigger breath before the phrase starts and hold some of it in reserve for that long note. Try it now. *Don't make me . . .*'

Jess took a deep breath and launched forth: '*Don't make me wait one more moment for my life to* start!' The wind whipped her voice away.

'Relax, and then do it louder and longer. Four counts to the key change and hold for four more.'

This time she did it and had breath to spare.

'See? When you relax a bit, it's easy.'

'Yeah, but it's not so easy in class. I mean,

I know you say I shouldn't go on about him, but look at Johnny! How am I supposed to follow a performance like that?'

Olly frowned and kicked at a pile of sodden leaves. 'Jess, can I tell you a secret? Johnny's a really good actor, but he's never going to change the world as a singer. Sure, he can do the voice and the moves and all that other cute stuff, but in the end an audience wants more. They wanna see who you are, as well as what you can do.'

'How do you know all this stuff?' asked Jess, zipping her tracksuit up to her chin.

'Because I'm super-wise. When you're up in your room, yacking away with Foxy and the rest of them, I'm staring out of the window in mine, figuring it all out.'

'So what should I do?'

'What I keep telling you. Think of singing as acting. Get into character as Tracy from *Hairspray* – really into character, like you did with that song from *Les Miz* – and then go for it.'

'Mmm, OK. I'll try.' She looked at him sideways. 'Can I ask you something? How're things with Spike?'

His eyebrows rose in surprise. 'Er . . . OK, I guess. Why do you ask?'

'Because she's my best friend ever, and she really likes you, and I don't want her to be hurt.'

He closed his eyes. 'Look, Jess, please . . . Spike can be hard to figure out, OK? She's not exactly your ordinary-type girl.'

The two of them stared at each other.

'Isn't that what you liked about her? That she's different? That she's special?'

'I'm just not sure what she wants,' muttered Olly.

'What every girl wants. Someone to make her feel loved and appreciated and, you know, all that stuff. She's got her friends and she's got her dancing, but . . . You're the wise one, Olly. Do I really have to spell it out?'

'No. I guess you don't.' He suddenly looked tired, as if he'd had something on his mind for a long time.' 'Look, Jess, I just don't think I'm the right person for her, right now.'

'OK. I think I understand. Sort of.'

'I don't think you do, but whatever. I'm really sorry.'

Jess frowned. 'Do one thing. Please. Be really nice to her for the next week, at least, and don't tell her what you've told me. She's got a big audition coming up and I want her to go into it feeling good.'

'Of course. I'll do that.'

'Just tell me one thing, though. Why did you spend all summer texting her? I mean . . . What did you want to happen? What did you *think* would happen?'

He closed his eyes. 'Let it go, Jess, OK?'

She nodded. 'I should get back. My ears are freezing. Like Shasha's.'

'Who's Shasha?'

'Ash's rabbit. Sorry, I'm not making sense. Gotta go. Thanks for the help with "Baltimore".' Her eyes watering in the wind, she marched back across the lawn. God, *boys*.

10

They were having lunch on Friday – macaroni cheese, which Jess wasn't crazy about, but which was supposed to be good for energy – when Miss Allen marched into the dining hall. She didn't need to signal for quiet; something in her manner spoke of the seriousness of her purpose, and the whole room fell silent as she took her place in front of them.

'I have just had two pieces of extremely worrying news,' she began. 'Shannon Matthews tells me that a valuable crystal bracelet has been taken from her room, almost certainly during the course of this morning. And Ricky Purkiss has reported the loss of his iPod, which he says was taken from his bag during morning classes yesterday. Now it pains me to suggest that any Arcadian is capable of stealing from his or her fellow students, but unless anyone has a better explanation –' she looked around the room, from table to table, but no one moved, or so much as blinked – 'it looks very much as if Shannon's bracelet and Ricky's iPod have been taken by one of you.'

Jess looked at Spike to see if she'd managed to lip-read everything Miss Allen had said. Spike's expression told her that she had. Both of them knew and liked Ricky Purkiss, a promising actor with a gift for comedy, and the twin brother of bunhead Paige.

'What makes this matter even more serious is that last month, as I'm sure most of you know by now, a fifty-pound note disappeared from Felicity Healey's tracksuit. I put up a notice about this at the time, hoping that the money had been misplaced, or would simply turn up, but . . . well, that hasn't happened.' Once again Miss Allen looked around the room, and once again it was as if a kind of paralysis had descended on the entire student body.

'If anyone finds either Shannon's bracelet, Ricky's iPod or Felicity's money,' she continued, 'they should hand it in to the school office straight away. Likewise, if any of you hear anything, *anything at all*, which could help us find out what has happened, you can speak to me, or to any of the teachers, in absolute confidence.'

Jess glanced furtively around her. No one quite

dared to meet anyone else's eye, in case it was taken as a sign of guilt. Foxy was expressionless, Ash was staring at the macaroni on her fork, and Spike was frowning with concentration as she tried to follow everything that the head teacher was saying. 'People think lip-reading's a kind of magic trick,' she'd once told Jess. 'But it isn't. It's just really hard work, and you always miss stuff.'

'This school is built on trust,' Miss Allen continued. 'Onstage, as actors, singers and dancers, you have to trust your colleagues to be there for you. And the same thing is true of your offstage lives. To steal from your fellow students is the ultimate betrayal of that trust, and no one who does so has any place here at Arcadia. So, while we look into this matter, please consider yourselves grounded. All of you. Unless someone comes forward with information leading to the recovery of some or all of these missing articles, nobody will leave the school grounds this weekend. Thank you.'

For ten seconds no one moved. In the pin-drop silence, Jess heard the double doors of the dining hall swing closed behind Miss Allen, followed by the diminishing clip of her heels. Then everyone started talking at once. As the hubbub rose, Shannon slipped into the hall, looking upset, before taking her place with Flick and Kelly at their usual table.

'This is totally bad news,' said Ash. 'Grounded!'

'Yeah, I was really hoping that Flick had just lost that money,' said Foxy.

'It's still possible that she did,' said Ash. 'And that Ricky's forgotten where he left his iPod, and Shannon just left her bracelet somewhere . . .'

Jess shook her head. 'Ricky, just possibly, but not Shannon. That bracelet meant a lot to her. She'd never just leave it lying around in a drama studio or whatever.'

Ash pushed cold macaroni around her plate. 'But whoever stole it could never wear it. It'd be recognized straight away. And Ricky's iPod too.'

'Which means,' said Foxy, 'that there's only one possible motive for taking them. To sell. Bet you could get quite a bit for that bracelet on eBay. Isn't it like a limited edition, or something?'

'Whatever,' said Jess, suddenly irritated by the whole subject. 'We're grounded, and I was really looking forward to going out this weekend.'

'Yeah. Me too,' said Ash. 'Hot chocolate with cream on top.'

'Walnut cake,' signed Spike feelingly.

'Those hench boys who hang out at the bus stop,' murmured Foxy.

'Yeah, *Gissa snog, Ginger . . .*' grinned Ash.

'Well, I think they're sweet,' said Foxy.

The following morning, by mutual agreement, the four of them slept through breakfast and lay in bed, half awake, listening to the radio and the rain pattering at the window. They might have been grounded, but it was still Saturday.

At ten thirty, Jess got up and pulled on a pair of shorts and a track top.

'Where are you *going*?' asked Foxy, her voice muffled by her pillow.

'For a run. Gotta get out.'

'But it's pouring,' groaned Foxy. 'Think about your hair! Ash, Spike, stop her.'

'Don't go, Jess,' murmured Ash. 'There, I tried.'

Spike rubbed her eyes. 'Go,' she signed. 'It's raining men!'

For the next hour, Jess ran round the school grounds, following the path beneath the dank, wet trees, and pushing herself hard against the cold and the rain and her own exhaustion. No one else was out except for Mr Dear, the elderly school gardener, who was moving barrowloads of shining gravel from his shed to the edge of the netball court. Every time Jess passed him she raised her hand, and he gave her a brief smile from beneath the dripping hood of his raincoat.

In her mind, she saw Johnny looking out of a boys' dormitory-block window. He would see her and, half-recognizing her, would run out into the rain after her. In films, guys spent a lot of time with rain running down their faces, telling girls how much they loved them. And the girls always looked kind of adorable, with their hair all over the place, crying and laughing at the same time, but somehow without their noses running uncontrollably, as Jess's did when she cried.

Not going to happen, Jess told herself. 'Forget him, forget him, forget him,' she whispered as she splashed along the path.

Why was the emotional side of her life, the boy-related side, so permanently out of control? It was great to have a part in the panto, her drama classes were going brilliantly, and she was scoring OK grades in dancing and singing. But this Johnny business . . . Oh my!

And not just the Johnny issue, but the Olly issue too. The last thing that Spike needed was sympathy, but behind her friend's fiercely independent front, Jess knew, she was vulnerable. You could see it when she danced, when the graceful lines of her body seemed to express a kind of longing – for love, for happiness, for escape from the silence that enclosed her.

Why didn't Olly want to go out with Spike?

Why couldn't he see what a lovely person she was? Was that whole texting business in the summer just an attempt to persuade himself that he was one of the guys, with an adoring girlfriend who sent him hearts and kisses?

And then there was Ash, trying her hardest to hold it all together, worrying about her upcoming Phoebe Skye audition in her secretive Ash-like way, and clearly longing for Zane to hit her with a text and make everything OK again. What had that boy told her, Jess wondered, pounding through a series of puddles so that the rainwater splattered up her bare legs. *Why do we allow these boys to dominate our lives and our thoughts and our dreams?*

As if there wasn't enough to worry about already – these thefts, for a start. No one knew what steps the school was taking to investigate them, but the teachers looked unusually serious, hurrying purposefully through the corridors after classes and disappearing into the office at odd hours in concerned-looking groups. Among the students, meanwhile, the drip, drip, drip of distrust ate away at friendships and poisoned the atmosphere.

Who would be the next victim, she wondered. Or was it all over? Maybe the thief had been scared off by all the fuss and the talk of investigation. In which case they'd never know who'd been responsible. But they'd wonder, and suspicions would be voiced and fingers pointed, and the distrust would never really go away.

As Jess crunched across the drive in front of the main building a long gust of wind strained at the trees, flattening her wet track top to her back. Her legs were tired now, and she could feel a knot of hunger tightening inside her, but after a quick glance in the direction of the dining hall she decided to drive herself on for one last circuit.

As if her failed love life and the thefts weren't enough to worry about, there was the whole thing with her mum, and the suggestion that she might suddenly arrive back from South Africa. As far as all that was concerned, Jess didn't really know what she felt. The perfect solution, of course, would be for her parents to get back together again, and for Creepy Eyebrows (her mum's deeply horrible boyfriend) and Elaine (her dad's actually quite nice girlfriend) to just kind of fade into history and gradually be forgotten.

But that wasn't going to happen. She was glad she'd made the effort with Elaine because her dad had been so grateful and, really, Elaine could have been a lot worse, all things considered. Perhaps it had helped that Jess first met her on that magical day at the end of the previous term. Remembering it, Jess swung off the path and ran through the woods to the amphitheatre. This outside auditorium, set in a clearing among the oaks and beeches, was where she had played Titania in *A Midsummer Night's Dream*. She came to a halt and slowly descended the arc of stone steps. That fragrant July evening seemed an age ago. Then, illuminated by lanterns and stage lights, and with its dance-floor and scenery in place, the amphitheatre had been a place of enchantment. Now, rainswept and deserted, it just looked bleak.

Remounting the steps, suddenly cold and tired, Jess jogged back through the gaunt trees towards the dorm block. Squelching into the locker room, she found Spike changing after a pointe-work session in one of the dance studios. She looked excited and upbeat.

'Have you seen Olly?' Jess asked.

Spike nodded, her eyes shining. 'Texted me. Said it was great about the audition. *Fingers crossed. Kiss, kiss.*'

Oh yeah, thought Jess. *God, I wish I'd never spoken to him. I'm deceiving my best friend, and I feel really, really mean.* But right now, with the *Nutcracker* audition coming up, she couldn't see what else to do. Spike had to go in there happy, confident and walking tall.

Leaving her sodden clothes in the changing room, Jess made for the showers. There was a grumbling sound, and tepid water hissed at her face. The next minute it turned ice cold, and then suddenly so hot that she had to dance backwards to avoid being scalded. Showers at Arcadia were always a bit of a hit-and-miss affair.

'Ash got a text too,' Spike told her fifteen minutes later as they were making their way upstairs to Room 10.

'Don't tell me,' said Jess. 'From Zane? The lovesick puppy?'

Spike nodded.

'He's taken his time.'

But Ash seemed pleased. 'He's had some issues to work out,' she explained vaguely.

'Yeah, "how to keep you on a string"-type issues,' said Foxy. 'He knows that all he's gotta do is call and you'll come running.'

'I will *not*,' said Ash.

'Maybe not running, but you'll get back with him,' said Jess, and Spike smiled her agreement.

'Two weeks,' she signed. 'Tops.'

'Thanks for the vote of confidence, guys,' said Ash.

Washing bag in hand, slippers on her feet, Foxy shuffled towards the door, her face thoughtful. 'Has anyone given any thought to the reason we're all stuck here today?' she asked. 'I mean, like who might have stolen Shannon's bracelet and Flick's money and Ricky's iPod? Because I'm beginning to wonder whether we shouldn't start worrying about our own stuff.'

There was a long silence.

'What do you think we should do?' asked Jess vaguely, flipping open her laptop to check her emails.

There were just two. One was from Spike. Entitled 'Anyone we know???' it was a link to a YouTube clip of a duck quacking the opening notes of a Phoebe Skye song.

The other was from her mother, and the subject box held the single word 'Hi!'.

For a moment, Jess stared at it. Then, with a flick of her finger on the trackpad, she exited and snapped the laptop closed. Whatever the message was, this wasn't the time to open and read it. She'd wait until she was alone.

II

Jess only had one real treasure, a slender gold necklace with a sapphire ring on it. It was the only thing that her mum had left her when she went. The ring was tiny, too small even for Jess's little finger, and Jess had no idea where her mum had got it from, but until she came to Arcadia she'd worn the necklace every day. Now, with all the endless changing of clothes for dance classes and sport, it lived in the toe of an old jazz shoe in her bottom drawer, along with a jumble of holey leg warmers and her netball kit. Everything else, including her phone and her purse, went into her dance bag, which she carried with her everywhere.

The other three made similar arrangements to be sure nothing precious was left around when they were out, and Jess guessed that elsewhere in the school people were doing the same – gathering together the things that were special to them and trying to hide them away. But this didn't prevent the next theft five days later. The victim was a second year named Emma Tucker, a pretty, popular girl whose rock 'n' roll voice and long chestnut hair Jess had always envied. Emma had done a sponsored walk during the summer holidays for one of the charities that Arcadia supported, and her mother had sent her the fifty-five pounds that she'd earned, so that she could give it to Miss Allen. The envelope, containing a letter and the cash, had been delivered on Thursday morning and put away in Emma's chest of drawers in Room 14. She had meant to take the money to the school office, but by the time she went to collect it from her room, that evening, it had gone.

No announcement was made, but the whole school knew that there had been another theft by lights-out time. And when Jess and the others walked into the dining hall for breakfast at seven thirty on Friday morning, the place was almost silent, with students huddled in tight, distrustful groups, whispering to each other and darting suspicious glances around them.

'I tell you,' said Ash, 'I'm glad we're all going up to London tomorrow. I really don't think I could spend another weekend shut up in this place. This whole business is totally getting to me.'

It was getting to everyone. Rumours flew about. A shadowy figure had been seen on the girls' dorm-block fire escape on Wednesday evening; Miss Allen was calling in private detectives to investigate the thefts; a first-year boy had been seen leaving the school office in tears. Every time a student was seen speaking to a member of staff, it was taken as evidence of a new twist in the plot. Girls hugged their bags to their sides, boys walked around with pockets bulging with their valuables. A talented but very spoilt dance student named Nina Nikanova, known to her fellow third years as Knickers, insisted on taking an entire overnight bag of her clothes from class to class. 'It's designer!' she told her exasperated teachers and anyone else who would listen.

Friday seemed to go on forever, but when classes were finally over Jess and Spike met for a chat and a coffee in the theatre green room. This was a kind of waiting room, below the stage, where performers could put their feet up while they waited to go on. The Arcadia green room was a dusty Ali Baba's cave, smelling of theatrical make-up and musty old costumes, and furnished with broken-backed sofas, gilt-framed mirrors and trunks full of swords, masks and pirates' boots. Although rarely cleaned it was always warm and dry, and there was usually a jar of

Nescafé on the tin tray beside the kettle. Today, happily, there was half a carton of milk and a bag of lumpy sugar there too.

As Jess was making the coffee, Calvin walked in with a first-year student, new that term, called Linnet Dunne. For a long moment Calvin stared at Jess, expressionless. Then, without speaking, he turned round and walked out again.

'Well, that was weird,' said Linnet apologetically. 'We were going to run through a scene from *Les Miz* together.'

'Sorry, 'fraid it might have been me,' said Jess. 'Calvin doesn't seem to be speaking to me right now.'

'Oh well,' said Linnet. 'Whatever! Since I'm here, do you guys mind if I stay and get on with my maths assignment?'

''Course not. Coffee?'

'Mmm, yes thanks, please!' She settled herself on one of the rickety sofas, next to the donkey's head that Olly had worn in A *Midsummer Night's Dream*, and opened her schoolwork bag.

'How are you enjoying it here?' Spike asked her, and Jess translated.

'Um, yeah, really loving it.' She grinned shyly at Spike. 'I've seen you dance. You are like, *majorly* good.'

'Do you like ballet?' Spike signed.

'It's OK. I'm not one of Miss Pearl's specials. I'm more into jazz dance and singing.'

'Sugar, people?' asked Jess, teaspoon poised over the Tate & Lyle bag.

She handed out the coffee. When she and Spike met here, they always used the same mugs. Spike's had a chip out of the rim, just above an illustration of Homer Simpson saying 'Doh!', and Jess's had a design of flying pigs. Both were ancient and tea-stained, relics of the 1990s, but there was something comforting about them. Something to do with all the Arcadians who had sat in this green room over the years and were now out in the world, earning their fortunes, or trying to.

'Are you nervous about the audition?' Jess signed when she saw that Linnet's attention was focused on her homework.

'Just hope I get it,' signed Spike.

'Would you like to join the English National Ballet?'

'That or the Royal. They both do the ballets I want to dance. *Swan Lake*, *Giselle*, *Romeo and Juliet* . . .'

Jess nodded and sipped her coffee, a little awed that her friend was thinking so far ahead. She herself had got no further than vague imaginings of heroines, possibly Shakespearean, in beautiful period costumes. And then, more private still (and never *ever* to be put into words), there was the movie fantasy, a montage of scenes which opened with her learning lines on the veranda of a beach house in California, and closed in a silent storm of flashbulbs at a London première. *Dream on, Jess*, she told herself. *Next stop Reading pantomime. And you're lucky to have that.*

'Why did your mum and dad send you here?' she asked Spike. 'To a mixed stage school, with singing and acting and stuff? Why not a ballet school?'

'My teacher in Scotland. She'd been in the Royal with Miss Pearl and told Mum and Dad she was the best teacher for me. And they thought I'd be happier here. Ballet schools can be quite stressy and intense.'

'No problem about you not doing the voice classes?'

Spike shrugged, and at that moment Linnet looked up from her books, worry clouding her face. 'Can I ask you guys something?'

They both nodded.

'How do you make a pie chart?'

Jess thought for a moment. 'Imagine a cheesecake . . .' she began.

12

'Well, it's a lovely morning for an audition,' said Miss Pearl cheerfully as the van nosed forward up the school drive. It was six forty-five, and still dark.

Beside Jess's face, rain blurred the window. Behind her, Paige had already fallen back asleep against Georgie's shoulder, her snores just audible against the whisper of Spike's earphones. Spike herself was awake, her eyes closed but her head nodding faintly to the hip-hop beat.

'How much of that can you actually hear?' Jess had once asked, seeing her scrolling through her playlist.

Spike had returned her phone to her pocket. 'Enough,' she signed.

'Sorry,' Jess murmured. 'Silly question.'

'It's not a silly question. It's just one I can't answer.' Spike shrugged. 'Being deaf, Jess – it's just a different way of going through life. It doesn't need fixing. *I* don't need fixing!'

And Jess had understood – that even if her friend's sound world was limited, the little that she heard, or sensed, filled her consciousness. It resonated; it had its own mystery and complexity. It was, as she said, enough.

Hunching into her rain jacket, cheek pressed against the window of the van, Jess closed her eyes. When she awoke it was light, the rain had stopped and Miss Pearl was pulling up outside a cafe on the outskirts of Reading. All seven girls were suddenly ravenous.

'Bacon sandwiches!' said Ash, five minutes later, when their breakfasts had arrived. 'Reminds me of that film set.'

'We were so lucky that day,' murmured Foxy.

'Let's hope we get lucky today,' said Poppy, stirring her tea.

'It won't be luck that gets you through, it'll be hard work,' said Miss Pearl. 'Just do your best, girls. And remember to *perform*. They'll be looking for people with personality. People who can project to the back of the theatre.'

'I'm worried about my hair,' signed Spike.

Jess translated for Miss Pearl.

'Well, a girl living in nineteenth-century Nuremberg probably wouldn't have had an asymmetric haircut,' the ballet teacher agreed.

'But it's too late to do anything about that now. If they offer you a part, you'll have to get it cut.'

'Should I tie a scarf round it?'

'No. It looks as if you've got something to hide. Go as you are, smile and be yourself.'

'Should we wear make-up?' asked Georgie.

'No,' said Miss Pearl firmly. 'You're supposed to look like children going to a Christmas party, not lap dancers.'

'Not even a smidge of lippy?' asked Poppy. 'All the other girls will.'

'No doubt they will,' said Miss Pearl. 'And that will be their first mistake.'

The rest of the journey seemed to take hours, and when they hit the rush-hour traffic outside London the van slowed to a crawl. Eventually they drew up at a long, low building in a cobbled street near the Albert Hall. A small crowd of dancers and teachers was waiting at the entrance, while a man with a clipboard ticked off names.

Miss Pearl ran through the timetable for the day. Georgie, Poppy and Paige were being picked up and taken out to lunch after the audition by Georgie's mother, who would then drive them back to Arcadia. Spike and her room-mates would go back in the van with Miss Pearl.

Looking over her shoulder from the driving seat, the dance teacher addressed Jess, Ash and Foxy. 'I'll see you back here at one o'clock. Do you know where you are?'

Foxy looked at her phone. 'We're going to Kensington High Street. It's about five minutes' walk away.'

Jess looked at Spike, who was nervously checking her pointe shoes, and then at Miss Pearl. 'Can I stay and watch the audition?' she asked.

'If the English National Ballet people don't mind, it's fine by me,' said Miss Pearl.

She spoke to the man with the clipboard, who nodded, and a couple of minutes later they made their way into an airy, light-filled ballet studio where close to a hundred people were milling about. Most of them were dancers, some in street clothes, some already changed and warming up at the barre that ran along three of the walls. A mirror ran the length of the fourth, in front of which an uneven line of chairs was drawn up. A sign in red marker pen pointed the way to the changing rooms. Leaving Jess with Miss Pearl, Spike and the other Arcadia girls hurried off.

'Serena Pearl!' The speaker was a trim, dark-haired figure with the sprightly posture of an ex-dancer.

'Juliet Dale!' The two women hugged. 'How lovely to see you! Are you . . .'

'Yes, I'm on the teaching staff here at the company. But you look fantastic, Serena. Still at Arcadia?'

'Yes, I've got four girls auditioning.'

The other woman turned to Jess. 'Your teacher and I were in the Royal together, several centuries ago. Old school tights, you see. Is she very strict?'

'Dreadfully!' confirmed Jess.

'I'm very glad to hear it. Are you auditioning?'

Jess shook her head and Miss Pearl explained that she'd come to support her friend Verity, and that Verity was deaf and needed to be able to see the person taking the audition, so that she could lip-read.

Juliet nodded. 'I'll get Vladimir to come and talk to you, and you can point your girl out to him.'

Vladimir, it turned out, was the company's ballet master. A slender, upright figure with a neat silver beard, he spoke English with a strong Russian accent.

'She deaf, you say, this girl. Ears not work?'

'No,' said Miss Pearl. 'Ears not work.'

'Then how she hear music?'

'She manages.'

'OK, we see if she manage. Which one?'

'Over there. In the silver-grey. With the hair.'

'Punk rock girl?'

'That's the one.'

'OK, I make sure she see me.' He indicated Jess. 'This girl audition too?'

'No,' said Miss Pearl. 'She's Verity's friend. Is it all right if we stay and watch?'

Vladimir shrugged. 'Is not usually allowed, but perhaps better you stay here in case I have problem with punk rock girl.'

He walked away and Jess surveyed the studio. There were about fifty dancers there, chatting, stretching and going through the usual pre-class rituals. Each one was wearing a number pinned to her leotard, front and back, and all of them, to Jess's eye, looked ferociously talented.

By the entrance, a haughty-looking woman in a fur coat was causing a scene. 'My daughter is *auditioning*,' she was saying in a loud, upper-class voice. 'I *insist* that I be allowed to stay.'

With a shock, Jess realized that the woman was a frightening forty-five-year-old version of Georgie. The Honourable Pamela Maxwell, no less. That her guess was correct was confirmed by the freaked-out look on Georgie's face, and her obvious relief when the woman was finally bundled out of the studio. *Honestly*, thought Jess. Auditioning was bad enough without a bonkers parent showing up and causing trouble. She was pierced by a sudden, sharp sense of loss. *Mum would never have embarrassed me like that. She wasn't perfect, but she knew the rules.*

If Jess had any lingering thoughts of becoming a dancer, coming to these studios would have dispelled them. The ballet girls were terrifying. Sleek and whippet-thin, they stalked around the studio with nervy purposefulness, each in her own fiercely determined little world. Following Miss Pearl's instructions, the four Arcadians had split up, rather than staying in a group. Spike was standing at the barre between a girl in a turquoise Elmhurst leotard and another in the dark blue of the Royal Ballet School. Apart from her, every single auditioner had her hair smoothed into a neat, regulation bun. Miss Pearl was right: that weird asymmetric cut of Spike's certainly drew the attention.

The audition started in the usual way, with exercises at the barre. By the time the dancers had reached the end of these, half an hour later, Jess had a fair idea of who the contenders were. Spike was among them, but the competition was stiff. In Miss Pearl's classes at Arcadia, the willowy Scottish girl stood out effortlessly. Here, everyone had ballet bodies – long necks, supple backs, legs turning out smoothly from the hips, beautifully arched feet.

When the dancers moved away from the barre into the centre of the studio, the differences between them became more obvious. Vladimir set the exercises at high speed, explaining them once only, and some of the girls got flustered. Steps were forgotten mid-sequence, turns were fluffed, jumps went the wrong way. Poppy, at one point, caused a mid-air collision, bringing down another girl who looked at Poppy as if she was ready to strangle her. Jess had never been happier just to watch, rather than taking part.

At the end of the hour-long class, Vladimir accepted the formal curtseys with which students traditionally thank their teachers, and left the studio. As the dancers paced uncertainly around, Juliet Dale, who'd been taking notes a couple of seats away from Jess, got to her feet.

'OK, girls,' she began. 'Thank you very, very much for coming today. We all know that auditions aren't the greatest fun in the world, but if you're to be dancers they will be part of your lives for the next few years at least. So what's going to happen now is that I'll read out a list of numbers. And if your number's not on that list, then I'm afraid that's it for today.'

The students looked around them, trying not to appear too worried, and went into tight little clusters with their schoolmates. Spike, Georgie, Poppy and Paige put their arms round each other.

'Right, here we go. If I call your number, please put your pointe shoes on. If I don't, please go through and get changed.'

'Five . . . nine . . . eleven . . .'

One by one, their faces blank, the rejected dancers left the room. Those whose numbers were called tried not to look too triumphant.

'Twenty-seven . . . twenty-nine . . .' One from Elmhurst, one from Tring. Number twenty-eight was Poppy, who snatched up her bag and left the studio without a backward glance.

'Thirty-two . . . Thirty-five . . . Thirty-six . . .' Georgie, Paige and a girl from the Royal Ballet School were through. Expressionless, they busied themselves with their pointe shoes.

'Thirty-nine . . . forty-three . . .' Spike was through.

'Well done, all of you,' said Juliet Dale, when the last of those who had been turned down had left the studio. 'We need two casts of eight and two covers for each cast. So you'll all be in the production.'

The dancers grinned at each other as they paced around. There were a couple of suppressed *woo-hoos*. One girl, frowning, put her hand up.

'Yes . . . Maria?' said Juliet, checking the girl's number against her list.

'Two casts of eight and four covers makes twenty. There are twenty-two of us here.'

'Well spotted, Maria. Anyone guess why?'

'You need two alternating Claras?' said another girl.

Juliet nodded. 'Exactly. Clara is the central character in *The Nutcracker*. Everything that happens, all the magical stuff, happens to *her*. So it's a major role, probably the most important juvenile role in the whole of classical ballet, and a big responsibility. Whoever we choose will be dancing with our ballerinas and lead male dancers. And that's what we're going to decide right now, so catch your breath, keep warmed up and be ready to go in five minutes.'

13

When Juliet Dale returned, it was with Vladimir and an elegant figure dressed entirely in black.

'That's Madame Tamara,' whispered Miss Pearl. 'She's the director of the company.'

As the two women took their places on the chairs in front of the mirror, Vladimir divided the dancers into groups and began to set the first routine, making sure that Spike could read his lips as he did so. 'We have deaf girl,' he explained to the other dancers, pointing at her. 'So give her chance, OK?'

The routine was clearly intended to test their pirouettes. Georgie and Paige were in the first group, and Jess could tell from their body language that, while they were pleased to have made it through the first stage of the audition, they didn't expect to get much further. Spike was in the third group, along with a dark-haired girl from the Royal Ballet School, who seemed able to do everything, effortlessly and beautifully. When Spike whipped off three pirouettes on pointe, number thirty-six sailed round for four, finishing perfectly and fixing her reflection in the mirror with a cool little smile.

And there were others, equally dangerous. One of the Elmhurst girls had an instinctive musicality that drew Jess's attention to her every time she danced. There were two Japanese girls, both very pretty, who could do everything. And there was a speedy little redhead and a super-flexible black girl, who must both have been from the English National Ballet School, since Vladimir addressed them by name.

After the pirouettes, he set a very fast sequence, all flickering footwork and lightning changes of direction. Jess watched with her fingernails digging into the palms of her hands. Spike could do the routine, but this kind of dancing was not her strong point. Like the black girl, she was just too long-legged. The little redhead, by contrast, flew through it, as did the girl from the Royal, her feet skimming the floor, and her face set in that demure, catlike smile.

After the exercise, Madame Tamara stood up and fixed the dancers with a velvety gaze. 'Thank you all very, very much. You've done extremely well. I'd like just seven of you to stay behind. The rest of you, I'll see you at rehearsals next month.' And she read out a list of numbers that didn't include thirty-two or thirty-five. With something like relief, and a quick wave at Spike, Georgie and Paige left the studio. *Poor Poppy*, thought Jess. *Not nice to be the one left out.* Still, with a bit of luck, the Honourable Pamela would give them all a good lunch.

The surviving dancers looked at each other warily, hands on hips, sweat darkening their leotards. Spike stared straight in front of her, her face expressionless. She looked miles away but actually, Jess knew, she was thinking hard, calculating the odds.

'Time for names,' said Vladimir. 'Paula and Francine I know,' he nodded at the redhead and the black girl. 'But others, you tell me.'

'OK, I'm Giselle,' said the student from the Royal, demurely fluttering her eyelashes.

Oh please, thought Jess. *You have to be just the most annoying person alive. I hope you fall flat on your bum.*

'I'm Cathy,' said the Elmhurst girl.

'Ayako,' said the taller and very slightly prettier of the two Japanese girls.

'So you, Punk Rock, what your name?'

Spike stared at him.

'Voice not work either?'

She shook her head.

'Her name is Verity,' said Miss Pearl, quietly but clearly.

'OK then, Verity, Ayako, Cathy, Giselle, Paula, Francine – you show me what you can do.' He began setting the next sequence. '*Jeté à la seconde, developpé à la seconde* . . .'

'*Don Quixote*, Act 2,' whispered Miss Pearl. 'He wants to see if they can jump.'

But Jess could see that something was wrong. While demonstrating the steps Vladimir had forgotten to direct his words towards Spike and had turned away, so that she couldn't see what he was saying. Now she was staring worriedly at his back.

Suddenly he turned. 'OK, let's go. Giselle, Verity, you first.'

Giselle glanced at Spike, hesitated for a moment, then raised her hand.

'What is it?' demanded Vladimir irritably.

'Verity couldn't see what you were saying. She didn't get the steps.'

Spike looked at Giselle. Nodded her thanks. Giselle gave her the ghost of a wink.

The Russian looked at them. 'OK,' he said flatly. 'I repeat.'

Jess bit her lip. Shame washed over her at her earlier, unkind thoughts about the Royal Ballet

School girl. The pianist started to play, and Spike and Giselle launched into the *Don Quixote* solo.

As dancers, the two girls were polar opposites. If Spike was airy, Giselle was steely. While Giselle danced on the music, hitting the beat each time, Spike seemed to be carried along by it. Where Giselle had precision, Spike had flow.

'They're so different,' Jess whispered.

'Chalk and cheese,' Miss Pearl agreed. 'Glad I don't have to choose between them.'

Cathy and Paula went next. Here the contrast was even more pronounced, but to Jess's eye the Elmhurst girl had the edge over the redhead, whose dancing looked a little tense. Of the other two, Ayako was marginally the stronger, technically speaking, but Francine was more expressive.

Madame Tamara sat for a moment, considering, and then leant forward in her chair.

'OK, I just want to say that I think you're all lovely, in your different ways. But we have to make a choice, so I'm going to ask you all to show me this solo again, just once more, by yourselves. I know you're tired, but that's ballet for you. So give it everything you've got. Paula, you go first.'

The red-haired girl nodded and took her preparation. Her performance was faultless, but, as before, a little strained. Cathy followed Paula, and was followed by Francine and Ayako. Tiredness was beginning to tell, and both Cathy and Francine wobbled on their pirouettes. Ayako was technically perfect, but forgot to smile until the final bars of the music. After each girl danced, the others clapped encouragingly.

Spike and Giselle looked at each other. Neither of their expressions changed, but something indefinable passed between them – an acknowledgement that this, essentially, was between the two of them. That while they were rivals, at heart they were the same. Each, in the unblinking gaze of the other, saw her own ambition reflected straight back at her.

Giselle went first. Pressure clearly brought out the best in her, and her dancing was light, precise and detailed, with beautifully defined jumps and faultless pirouettes. Even during the final section of multiple turns, a sequence so difficult it made Jess's blood run cold, her catlike smile never faltered. When she finished, the four girls who had already danced applauded generously. Spike clapped too, but her face was unreadable.

Jess knew that she was figuring out how to beat the Royal Ballet School girl. Technically speaking, Giselle was untouchable, so Spike had to find an angle – a way of making her own performance unforgettable. For a moment she stood there, then she turned to the pianist and, with down-pressing movements of her hands, indicated that he should slow down the music.

Vladimir's eyebrows rose in surprise – it was unheard of for auditioning students to issue musical directions – and Jess heard Madame Tamara's amused intake of breath. Spike took an unhurried preparation and, with the opening notes of the music, launched into her first leap.

It was huge. She seemed to sail through the air in a high, smooth curve, landed gracefully and rose on to pointe, her other leg unfurling beside her. Holding the position for a heartbeat before allowing the leg to fall, she repeated the sequence to the other side. Leap followed soaring leap, balance followed balance, and as the solo unfolded Jess was conscious of her dance teacher sitting absolutely motionless beside her. Miss Pearl, it seemed, wasn't even breathing. And then suddenly it was over. Spike held her final position a few seconds longer, her arms held high, framing her face, and then, with the faintest of smiles, lowered them.

Again, the other auditioners clapped, and Spike shrugged and smiled and ran a hand through her hair. Jess could tell that she was pleased. That it had gone just about as well as it possibly could.

'Do you reckon she's got it?' she whispered.

'We'll soon know,' murmured Miss Pearl as

Madame Tamara and her colleagues conferred. After a minute or so, during which the dancers exchanged their pointe shoes for furry slippers and Ugg boots, the director rose and stepped forward. 'OK, well done, all of you. The standard was exceptionally high, but we've made our choice for our two Claras. First cast Giselle, second cast Verity. Thank you.'

As the other four girls stuffed their shoes into their bags and began to make their way to the changing room, Spike and the Royal Ballet School girl looked at each other with a mixture of uncertainly, exhaustion and sheer relief. Discreetly, they bumped fists.

'Well done, Serena,' said Juliet Dale, walking over to where Jess and Miss Pearl were sitting. 'Your girl's lovely. A credit to you. And the others are very promising too.'

'Well, thank you, Juliet, this'll be very good for them.'

'You must be so proud of your friend,' Juliet said to Jess.

'I am,' replied Jess. 'I think she's amazing. They all are. I'm totally in awe.'

Standing up, she realized that, once again, she was ravenously hungry. A little unsteadily, she walked over to where Spike and Giselle were figuring out how to communicate with each other.

Spike grinned, still excited from the audition. 'Tell her I'm impressed,' she signed.

Jess did so.

'Awww, thanks,' said Giselle. 'Me too. You're really good.' She took a pen and paper from her bag, wrote down a number and handed it to Spike. 'Text me, yeah?' And with a quick smile she swept up her things and was gone.

Ten minutes later Miss Pearl had made all the necessary arrangements concerning the *Nutcracker* rehearsals, and she and Spike and Jess were ready to leave the building. Georgie, Paige and Poppy, it seemed, had already left with the Honourable Pamela.

And then, suddenly, there at the entrance were Ash and Foxy, and for some reason Foxy was holding an enormous rough-coated dog. Like an oversized greyhound, and with an up-for-anything look in its eye it panted excitedly at the end of a plaited leather lead.

Spike, Jess and Miss Pearl stood there in amazement. Then a smile split Spike's face. Running forward, she threw her arms out and the dog, as if recognizing a long-lost friend, leapt up to meet her, dropped its huge paws on her shoulders and started licking her ear.

Miss Pearl stared at the two of them and then blinked. 'Eleanor, what exactly is –'

'It's a dog, Miss Pearl.'

'Yes, Eleanor, I did guess that much, but . . .'

'A mongrel,' Ash added helpfully. 'Mostly Scottish deerhound.'

'I see. And what *exactly* is this mongrel dog doing here with you?'

'It's ours,' said Foxy. She glanced at Jess. 'A man gave him to us.'

'A man,' said Miss Pearl flatly.

'Yes. Outside McDonald's. His name's Mungo.'

'The man's name was Mungo?'

'No, the dog's name is Mungo. The man didn't tell us what his name was.'

Miss Pearl closed her eyes and shook her head. Equally curious, anxious to follow the conversation, Spike gently lifted the dog's paws from her shoulders.

'Spike got a lead role in *Nutcracker*,' said Jess. 'Spike and a girl from the Royal Ballet School. Paige and Georgie got through too.'

Whooping and high-fiving, Ash and Foxy closed in on their friend. Keen to join in, Mungo jumped up at her too, making excited whiffling sounds.

'Eleanor!' said Miss Pearl, her voice cutting through the din. 'Ashanti! Will one of you please tell me what this dog is doing here?'

'OK,' began Foxy. 'What happened was this . . .'

But at that moment Paula, the red-haired English National Ballet School girl, stepped out of the building, followed by Ayako and several others. Seeing Spike and Mungo, Paula's eyes widened in delight. 'What a lovely dog. Is he yours?'

Spike shook her head and pointed at Foxy.

'He's *gorgeous*,' said Paula. 'Can I show him to my friends?' And, without waiting for an answer, she darted back into the building, followed by Francine, Ayako and several others.

'Can we stroke?' asked Ayako.

In seconds, more than a dozen ballet students were surrounding the dog, oohing and aahing and stroking and chattering loudly to each other. Mungo, thrilled to be the centre of attention, sat back on his haunches, panting happily.

A trio of very handsome men arrived, speaking rapid Spanish and laughing a lot. From their walk and posture Jess could tell that they were professional dancers and guessed they were company members. She knew she was right when several of the students broke off from cooing over Mungo, pulled out their phones and asked if they could pose for photos with them.

The men obliged, and somehow Spike and Mungo and Foxy were pulled into the frame too. As one of the dancers lifted Spike effortlessly to his shoulder, the dog leapt after her with such force that Foxy dropped the lead. Ash and Jess both dived for it but Mungo easily sidestepped them, snaking excitedly between the dancers before racing round in ever-widening circles, his paws skittering on the cobblestones.

From her vantage point, Spike nervously surveyed the chaos. Next to her, on another dancer's shoulder, Paula was shrieking with laughter and striking flirtatious ballet poses. 'Cubans are the best partners, no?' shouted the third dancer, swinging Ayako back and forth as her friend snapped away.

Spike didn't hear him. Nor did she hear Paula's laughter, or the hip-hop track that Francine had started playing on her phone, or Mungo's excited yelping as Jess, Foxy and Ash raced desperately after him. But she did see the look on Miss Pearl's face. And the door to the studios opening, and Juliet Dale appearing, followed by Madame Tamara.

The director didn't utter a single word, but the effect was instantaneous. Everyone froze. The hip-hop recording trailed into silence and the Cuban dancers slowly lowered their partners to the cobbles. Even Mungo stopped dead in his tracks, so that Foxy was able to grab the lead. Within seconds the crowd had dissolved, leaving the Arcadia group alone on the cobblestones.

Madame Tamara looked at Spike, her dark eyes thoughtful. 'What you did this morning was exceptionally smart, Verity. And under pressure too. I can see that you've been very well taught.' She inclined her head respectfully in the direction of Miss Pearl, who returned the gesture.

'We'll see you next month,' said Juliet. 'Nice dog, by the way, Serena!'

Miss Pearl opened her mouth to answer but the two women had already disappeared back into the building. Wearily, she turned to Ash and Foxy. 'So. You were telling me . . .'

What had happened, it turned out, was that Ash and Foxy had decided to visit McDonald's for a mid-morning snack. Nothing major, just a little something to keep them going between breakfast and lunch. They had been standing at the door, about to go in, when they'd been approached by a neatly dressed man holding Mungo. Could they possibly look after the dog while he ordered some food, the man asked, since dogs were not allowed into the restaurant. Ash and Foxy had looked at each other a little uncertainly – both were well aware of the dangers of getting into conversations with strangers – but the request had seemed harmless enough. And Mungo looked like a friendly dog.

So for a few minutes, as the man queued up

inside, the two girls had talked to Mungo, and stroked his rough black and silver coat, and agreed that if they were ever going to own a dog it would have to be a dog exactly like this one. Mungo, they decided, was pretty much perfect.

Eventually the man came out, carrying a burger and a packet of fries. 'So what do you think of him?' he asked.

'He's lovely,' they assured him.

'Well,' said the man. 'He's yours if you'd like to have him.'

And there, on the steps, as he ate his fries, he'd explained that he could no longer afford to keep Mungo. That he was going to take him to the dogs' home, where if no new owner could be found – and this would be difficult in London, given Mungo's size – he would be put to sleep.

The girls had looked at each other, horrified. And with that the man had fed Mungo his burger, explaining to Ash and Foxy that as it was the last meal he'd be able to give him he wanted to make it a special one.

'Come on, boy,' he'd said gently as the dog swallowed the last mouthful. 'Best to get it over with.' And he'd started to lead Mungo away.

Ash and Foxy had looked at each other, their eyes filling with tears. They couldn't remember which of them had first shouted 'Wait!'

'I see.' Miss Pearl nodded. 'And so here he is.'

'Here he is,' agreed Foxy, stroking Mungo's huge, hairy head.

Miss Pearl looked at the four of them, not unkindly. 'You know, don't you, that we'll have to take him to a dogs' home? That we can't possibly keep him.'

Ash looked at her imploringly. 'Please, Miss. Couldn't he live at the school? Other schools have a dog.'

'Ashanti, look at the *size* of him! I've seen smaller ponies. I can't just ring Miss Allen and say that you and Eleanor have found this . . . this giant dog, and that we're bringing it back. She'll think I've gone completely mad. And that you have too.'

'Will you just ask her?' begged Foxy, kneeling down on the cobbles and putting her arms round Mungo's neck. Sorrowfully, Spike did the same.

'If he goes to a dogs' home, nobody will want him,' pleaded Ash, close to tears. 'He's too big to live in a London flat. They'll have to put him to sleep.'

'Ashanti, that's not what happens, I promise you. They'll find a home for him, I'm sure of it.' But a tiny note of uncertainty had crept into Miss Pearl's voice, and Jess could see that the teacher was hesitating. It was now or never. *Act*, she told herself. *Act*.

Forcing herself to think of Mungo's fate – of the big, trusting dog led unknowingly to his doom – she made the tears come. Felt the first roll hotly down her cheek, and then the second. 'Please, Miss Pearl,' she sniffed. 'Let us take him back.'

'Please!' signed Spike.

Miss Pearl looked from face to imploring face. Then she turned away, took out her phone and moved out of earshot. The conversation lasted several minutes, with the four girls watching her every nod and head shake. Finally she returned, her expression stern.

'Well, I've spoken to Miss Allen. I told her first that Verity had been chosen, from among fifty of the most talented young dancers in the country, to share the role of Clara in *The Nutcracker*. Miss Allen was very pleased indeed and wants me to pass on how proud the school is of her.'

Foxy, Ash and Jess gathered round Spike, hardly daring to breathe, and Mungo wagged his tail enthusiastically.

'As regards the dog,' Miss Pearl continued levelly, 'I explained the situation as best I could. I told her that Mungo is very large, but appears to be of good character. She asked if I thought that he was likely to bite any of the students, and I said that, on balance, I didn't.'

'And . . .' whispered Ash.

'Her answer was that, given the recent upheavals in the school, a dog might – *just might* – be a good idea. A distraction.'

As one, the four girls leapt in the air, whooping. Startled, Mungo reared on to his hind legs, but this time Foxy remembered to keep hold of the lead.

'Miss Allen is prepared to have him on a month's trial,' Miss Pearl continued. 'He will live in the main building. If everything works out, and Mungo behaves himself, he can stay. But if there's the slightest trouble . . .'

'There won't be,' Jess breathed as they crowded round Mungo. 'We promise you.'

Miss Pearl shook her head. 'I have to say, you four are the most shamelessly manipulative girls I have ever met. And that includes the Royal Ballet. Now did someone mention lunch?'

14

When they returned to the school, shortly after six o'clock, most of the students were in the dining hall.

'You'd better let that dog have a run before we introduce him to Miss Allen,' said Miss Pearl. 'She's not going to be very pleased if the first thing he does is wee all over the office carpet.'

They tumbled out of the van and, a little hesitantly, Jess let Mungo off the leash. He bounded off and within seconds had vanished into the darkness. The girls gave chase and caught up with him by the boys' dorm block. Seeing them, Mungo rushed off again.

The four of them looked at each other. 'We'll never catch him,' said Ash.

'I think we should just wait here,' said Jess. 'He'll find us.'

At that moment the door to the dorm block opened behind them, and a figure stood silhouetted against the entrance. At first Jess didn't recognize him.

'Hi, Johnny,' said Foxy.

'Foxy. Guys. What're you all doing here?'

'Waiting for our dog,' said Ash.

'Dog?'

'We found a dog in London,' said Jess. 'A man was giving him away. Miss Allen said we could bring him back.'

A grey shadow came loping down the path. 'And here he is,' said Ash. 'Johnny, meet Mungo.'

'Wow,' breathed Johnny, reaching out a hand to the dog as Jess reattached the lead. 'You are *beautiful*.'

'Sit,' Jess commanded, dropping to one knee, and Mungo obediently sank back on his haunches. Coming closer, Johnny ruffled the dog's wiry grey hair.

'You say someone was *giving him away*?'

Jess began to tell him the story, conscious as she did so of the others looking at each other and, one by one, slipping away. Until the two of them were alone.

Reaching behind him, Johnny pushed the dorm-block door shut. They were in near darkness now, with Mungo panting between them, and the paving stone hard and damp beneath the knee of Jess's jeans. *Get up*, she told herself, her heart pounding. *This is a bad idea. A really bad idea.* But instead she knelt there, motionless, her hand on the dog's warm neck.

And then Johnny was beside her, stroking Mungo's head and ears in such a way that, after a time, he was stroking Jess's hand too. She turned to him, a look of enquiry on her face. It seemed like minutes passed, but it was probably only seconds before Mungo turned his head and started enthusiastically licking their faces.

'Whoa,' murmured Johnny, springing back and laughing.

Jess stood up, pulling Mungo to his feet. She felt dizzy, and the distant lights of the dining hall were blurred. 'Sorry,' she muttered. 'But this isn't going to happen.'

'Why not?'

'Because you're going out with Shannon, for a start.'

He sighed. 'Look, Jess, that whole thing . . . You're different, OK?'

Mungo lunged at something in the darkness and, with difficulty, she pulled him back. 'So what's that mean, Johnny? We're different, so you can have both of us?'

'No, it just means . . . that you're different.'

'As in, she's a model, and I'm . . . what, exactly?'

'As in, you're my Titania.'

'Johnny, get real. That was months ago. We were acting. And Shannon was your Titania too, if you remember.'

'I do. And I remember that she was very beautiful too.' He reached over and touched her cheek. 'But you were magic, Jess.'

She looked up at the outline of the trees, black against the dark grey of the sky. 'I have to go,' she told him. 'Miss Pearl and the others are waiting for me.'

Johnny shook his head and seemed about to speak, but Jess was already leading the dog back through the wet grass towards the main building. If Johnny had followed her, she didn't know what she'd have done, but he let her go.

'What a day,' sighed Foxy, who was lying on her bed with a used tea bag over each eye, a favourite beauty treatment of hers.

'Yeah,' yawned Ash. 'Spike's audition, Mungo, and now Jess and Johnny. Almost too much excitement.'

'Look, it really wasn't anything with Johnny,' said Jess. 'I told you because you're my best friends and I didn't want to *not* tell you, but basically . . .'

'I think he really likes you,' signed Spike.

Jess shrugged. 'Maybe he does, maybe he doesn't.'

'So if he broke up with Shannon . . . ?' asked Ash.

'He's not going to break up with Shannon,' said Jess.

'You know what I think,' said Foxy, lying with her head motionless on her pillow so as not to displace the tea bags. 'I think he would break up with Shannon if he dared. But he knows what trouble it would cause. They're like Arcadia's alpha couple, those two. Imagine what Shannon would say if he started all that "need some time apart" and "it's not you, it's me" type stuff. She'd go crazy. She'd literally tear him apart.'

'Foxy's right,' said Ash. 'She's got him pinned down.'

'Oh come on, guys,' protested Jess. 'You're making it sound like it's some sort of hardship to go out with her. The truth is that she's super-gorgeous and smart and probably quite nice to be with, in that Shannon-ish way of hers. Why wouldn't he want to stay with her?'

'You know something interesting?' said Foxy. 'In ancient Egyptian, the word for teenage boy is the same as the word for baboon.'

'Is that true?' asked Ash doubtfully.

'It's totally true. For example, you know Tutankhamen? His name means airhead. They called him that because he only ever went out with models.'

'Nothing changes,' said Jess. She came to a sudden decision – *can't put it off forever* – and pulling her laptop from its bag, cleared a space for it among the hairslides, chapsticks and scrunchies on her chest of drawers. A couple of clicks, and there was the message from her mum.

Darling Jess,

How are you, and how are things at your lovely school? It seems like a hundred years since we last saw each other, and I'm sure you're quite the actress by now! As you know, a career on the stage was something I always dreamt of, but life turned out otherwise, as life has a habit of doing.☹

Here in South Africa, I'm afraid that things are not so good. By which I mean that my relationship with Derrick has not worked out quite as I hoped. He has certain problems for which I can no longer take responsibility, and to cut a long and rather unhappy story short I am planning to draw a line under my life here and return to good old England.

So, darling Jess, this is where you come in! I need you to tell me what the situation is with this person Elaine!!! Is your father still seeing her and is it serious? I wouldn't want to cause problems!

So just email me, sweetheart, and give me a heads-up. No need to mention anything to Dad at this stage!!

Love always, Mum xxx

15

Miss Allen was right, Mungo did cheer things up at Arcadia. 'I can't think why we didn't get a dog earlier,' she told everyone. '*Such* good company.' He took up residence in the school office, in a large wicker basket next to the desk of Mr Dye, the school secretary. Here he would lie, his long legs hanging over the side, graciously receiving his many visitors. Twice a day he would be taken out for galloping circuits of the grounds, a task so popular among the students that a list had to be drawn up to prevent arguments. And after school breakfast and tea he would pad to the kitchens, where a large bowl of leftovers would be waiting for him.

Mungo wasn't choosy – he liked pretty much everyone – but his favourite walker was Spike. Whenever she was near his nose would twitch, and he would eagerly bound off to find her. Spike loved the big dog as much as he did her; after all, as Ash pointed out, they were both Scottish.

On the Friday after the audition, Jess and the others were watching TV in the dorm block, relaxing after a long afternoon in the science lab. 'Human biology,' sighed Foxy. '*So* gross.' The common room was busy, with girls reading magazines, nodding along to music and learning lines for upcoming drama classes. Poppy Rattigan, who had recovered from her upset at the audition, was sitting cross-legged on the floor, texting.

Jess was half asleep in one of the threadbare armchairs, a mug of tea undrunk on the floor beside her. The common room was the only really warm place in the whole block, and the voices on the TV had become a vague, background drone. So at first she didn't notice when the door opened and Zane walked in, self-consciously running a hand through his unruly blond hair. When Spike nudged her, though, Jess sat up with a start.

'I hope that's for me!' Emma Tucker called out, emptying a packet of Jaffa Cakes on to a plate, and Jess saw that Zane was carring a pink rose, almost certainly from the flower bed outside Miss Allen's office. Like his hair and clothes, it was wet with rain.

'Actually, I'm looking for . . . Ah, there she is.' He zeroed in on Ash. 'Can I, like . . . have a word with you? In private?'

As he stood there, rain jacket dripping, Jess

watched a series of emotions cross Ash's face. In the background, the TV went on jabbering away. Eventually Ash stood up. 'Come on,' she said, leading him out of the room.

'No going upstairs, Zane,' Emma shouted after them. 'That's girl country.'

Five minutes later, Ash came back into the common room, alone. She looked pleased, flustered and a little self-conscious, and she was carrying the rose.

'Surprise, surprise,' said Foxy.

'Oh come on, guys,' said Ash, tucking the rose behind one ear and helping herself to a Jaffa Cake.

Spike smiled. 'Like I said, two weeks!' she signed, and lifted her hand for a high-five with Jess.

'Did you tell him about the Phoebe Skye job?' asked Foxy.

'I haven't got the job yet, and the chances are I'm not gonna get it,' said Ash. 'But yeah, as it happens, I did mention it. Doesn't change anything, though, cos he'll be doing the panto with you guys.'

'And who knows what'll happen there?' said Jess dreamily. 'All those parties . . .'

'Calvin's doing the panto, isn't he?' asked Emma with the ghost of a smirk.

Jess rolled her eyes. 'Oh please. Don't you start.'

'Look, I'm not even thinking that far ahead,' protested Ash. 'I told Zane: *You want me back? You gotta earn it.*'

Catching Jess's eye, Spike smiled. Success in the *Nutcracker* audition had given her spirits a much-needed lift. She and Giselle exchanged texts regularly, and this new friendship seemed to mean a lot to her. Jess was pleased. She knew that Spike's life wasn't easy, and that talent was not the same thing as happiness.

And that was why she felt so bad when, a few days later, Olly caught up with the four of them as they left the dining hall.

His expression unreadable, he touched Spike on the arm. *He's going to tell her,* Jess thought, as the two of them dropped back. Why was life so unfair? Why did she have to stand back and watch her friend being hurt?

'What's with those two?' Foxy asked. 'That didn't look like good news.'

Jess shrugged, unwilling to let on that she had talked to Olly. And when Spike walked into the room and, without looking at any of them, threw herself face down on her bed, Jess stayed silent.

16

Jess didn't answer her mother's email. What could she possibly say? Either way she was trapped. If she said that her dad and Elaine seemed happy, her mum might feel that she had to stay away and, difficult though her mum was, that would break Jess's heart.

More than anything else, she wanted to speak to her dad, to ask him what he felt. But since her mum had asked her not to, this would be a kind of betrayal. And if she told her mum the strict truth, which was that sometimes her dad seemed happy and sometimes he didn't, that would be another kind.

The whole thing tied Jess in knots. She longed to talk to Spike about it, but Spike wasn't in a mood to communicate with anyone. She was keeping her eyes down and trying to dance the hurt away in the ballet studio. Jess knew the time would come when the two of them would discuss everything, but that moment was not yet.

And somehow she couldn't face talking about her parents to Ash and Foxy. Not because her room-mates wouldn't have been there for her, anxious to help, but because if she told them she'd never be able to escape the issue. It would come up every time she walked into the room. And, really, she just didn't want to think about it that often. It was all too . . . complicated.

In the end, she talked to Shannon. In a weird way, she trusted her. The two of them weren't friends, but they respected each other. And Jess knew that the other girl had been through difficult times with her own parents.

She caught Shannon after a singing class and they went to the dining hall, which wasn't the most cheerful place in the school but was one of the warmest.

'So how's the modelling going?' Jess asked her.

Shannon shrugged her shoulders inside her Abercrombie hoodie. 'Miss Allen told the agency I couldn't miss classes to do castings, so kinda slowly, I guess. But I'm doing some editorial for *Tatler* at Christmas, which is cool.'

Jess wasn't quite sure what editorial was, and she'd never opened a copy of *Tatler*, but it sounded impressive. 'That is cool,' she agreed.

Shannon leant forward, her blue eyes narrowing, and hooked a tress of honey-blonde hair behind her ear. 'So what is it, Bailey? Come to ask if you can borrow my boyfriend again?'

Jess stared at her, speechless.

'Oh come on, Jessica. I know that you and Johnny have this flirty little . . . *thing* going. But I wouldn't want you to get hurt, because it doesn't mean anything. He's not going to leave me.' She angled her head, so the pale autumn light caught the soft line of her cheekbone. 'I mean, why would he?'

Jess said nothing.

Shannon smiled. 'You *are* hurt, aren't you? Well, Earth calling Jessica, he couldn't care less. It's a game he plays, taking – no offence – ordinary-looking girls and making them fall for him. You're not the only one crying over Johnny, believe me.'

'If that's true . . .' Jess took a deep breath, her head spinning. 'Why do you . . . why do you stay with him?'

'Because he's a super-cute guy, Jessica. And I'm, y'know, *me*! Is it forever? I doubt it. But for now, hey! Who else is there?'

'So you don't . . .'

'Love him? I'm not *that* stupid.' She twitched her sleeves up her arms. 'Look. Jessica. I don't know why you're here, or what you want out of life. To *act*, I'm guessing. Well, so do I. But by acting I don't mean doing some dreary fringe thing that no one wants to see, or competing with a hundred other losers for a walk-on in a TV soap. I mean feature films. Lead roles. I have a plan, and the modelling's just the beginning of it. Have you got a plan, Jessica?'

Jess shook her head.

'Well, let me suggest something. Start as you mean to go on. Think of yourself as a star, and that's how people will treat you.' She shrugged. 'It's not complicated. Ask your friend Foxy. She'll tell you the same thing.'

Jess very much doubted that Foxy would do anything of the sort, but she said nothing.

'Look, Jess, boys like you. You've got, I don't know, *something*. So work on it. Stop grunging around in that hoodie. Sort your hair out. Get a grip.' She leant forward. 'Making people fall in love with you, Jess. It's fun, but it takes work. And it's something you need to practise, because that's how you get what you want.'

Jess shook her head. 'We're different, Shannon. I just don't work like that.'

Shannon shrugged. 'Well, don't say I haven't tried to help. What did you want to ask me about?'

Jess decided to proceed carefully. 'You know when your parents were like . . . having trouble.'

'Er . . . Yeah.'

'Did you ever find yourself caught between them?'

Shannon looked at her warily. 'Why are you asking me this?'

After a moment's hesitation, Jess told her everything. Derrick, Elaine, the emails, the way her mum was asking her to more or less spy on her dad. 'And I know that you've been through this sort of thing and I thought that you might have, y'know, some kind of advice?'

Shannon looked at Jess for a moment. 'This stays between us, yeah? You do *not* share it with your girl gang.'

Jess nodded.

'Your mum left, right? Went off with some other guy?'

Again, Jess nodded.

'In my case it was my dad. That thing people say: the magic had gone out of their marriage? Well, it was like that. Mum had kind of let herself go, stopped caring what she looked like, and Dad started seeing someone from work.'

Jess winced sympathetically.

'Yeah, it was a bad time. No one ever actually told me what was going on, but I worked it out, like you do.'

'So you weren't kind of . . . caught between them?'

'Not like that. Most of it happened while I was here at school.'

'But you know at the end of last term, when you went off with them . . .'

'Leaving you with my lead role in *Midsummer Night's Dream* and my boyfriend as your love interest? Yes, I just about remember that.'

'Shannon, what you did that day was the best thing that's ever happened to me, and I'll always owe you for that. But the thing I've never fully understood is . . . why?'

'Well, it wasn't to advance your career, Bailey.'

'I guessed that.'

Shannon smiled a little sadly, and for a moment the look in her eyes was that of someone much older than her fourteen years. 'I didn't have anything figured out,' she said. 'They arrived that morning – you remember it had been so wet, and suddenly it was this hot, hot day – and I could see that everything was kind of fragile between them. They said that things had been very difficult, like I needed to be told, but that they'd had counselling and wanted to give things another go. That we would start doing things much more as a family, blah-di-blah, you know the kind of stuff?'

Jess didn't, but she nodded anyway.

'So, anyway, I go off and do my Titania in the afternoon performance, and it goes brilliantly, as you know, since you were in it too. Some kind of fat little fairy, I seem to remember.'

'That's right.'

'And then afterwards I meet up with Mum and Dad, and they're more or less holding things together. But I begin to wonder whether it's such a good idea making them stand around for several more hours, just so's they can sit through me doing the whole performance again that evening. It would mean leaving the school very late, and with the early start to the airport the next day no one would get much sleep, and there would be arguments – you know what it's like, travelling with adults – and I could just see everything falling apart again. And then I realize. I've done my performance, and everyone's saying how fabulous I was, so why not quit while I'm ahead and my parents are still talking to each other. There's someone else who knows the part, after all.'

'The fat little fairy,' said Jess.

'Exactly. So off I go.'

'And on I go,' said Jess. She smiled. 'I'm just so, so grateful to you for giving me that chance.'

'Don't be,' said Shannon. 'You were supposed to fail.'

'*What?*'

'I thought you'd be rubbish as Titania. I thought

you'd freeze up, forget your lines and make a total fool of yourself; that's why I let you do it.'

Jess stared at her.

'Oh come on, Jessica. You don't think I'd have let you go on if I thought you'd be any *good*, do you?'

'Why?' she whispered. 'Why would you want to do that to me?'

'Why d'you think? You let Johnny kiss you and the whole school knew about it. How d'you think that made me feel? How d'you think that made me *look*? Letting you tie yourself in knots as Titania would have been the perfect revenge. But then – who knew? – you turned out to be good. And the reason I didn't really mind was that Mum and Dad managed to patch things up.'

'I . . . I'm glad,' said Jess, stunned by Shannon's frankness.

Shannon nodded. 'My advice is don't get caught in the middle of these parent fights. Email your mum and tell her you're not prepared to go behind your dad's back. Get tough.' She smiled. 'Tell her you've got enough drama in your life dealing with competitive bitches like me!'

17

Over the next few days, the subject of the thefts seemed to fade and a more normal atmosphere returned to the school. Spike was more subdued than usual as she sadly came to terms with the fact that she and Olly would never be an item, but Ash, it appeared, was happier. A naturally private person, she didn't share the details of her relationship with the others, but things with Zane looked as if they were back on course. What was more, he seemed to be treating her with a certain amount of respect since Ash had made it clear she wasn't prepared to have it any other way.

'Have you seen her when she's angry?' Zane whispered to Foxy in one of Mr Casey's drama classes. 'She's terrifying!'

'So don't make her angry,' Foxy snapped. 'Make her happy.'

'You're right,' said Zane. 'That's exactly what my strategy's gonna be.'

After some thought, and following her conversation with Shannon, Jess replied to her mum's email.

It's fantastic news that you're coming back. And sorry things haven't worked out, but it would be SO great if you could be part of my life again. Things are a bit up and down at school right now but I've got some lovely friends, specially my room-mates, and we all try to help each other out. Boyfriend-wise there just isn't the time, but who knows what the future might hold!!! I'm only 14, in case you've forgotten (joking) so there is time! The work is tough (loving the acting most) and I've been chosen to be in a pantomime at Xmas which is quite a big deal (Theatre Royal, Reading!!!), and mostly thanks to Miss Julie and all those years of tap, jazz, etc. at the church hall. About Elaine you'll have to ask Dad as honestly I have no idea and wouldn't want to go behind his back. Sorry but know you'll understand, your loving (semi-professional!) showbiz legend daughter xxx *JESS*

That should do it, she mused, clicking Send.

The calm at the school didn't last. There was

another theft, and the victim was none other than Johnny Finn. Once again, the announcement was made when the whole school was in the dining hall. Johnny's wallet, Miss Allen told the assembled students, had disappeared from his jacket, which he had briefly taken off in the theatre. There had been money in it, as well as photographs 'of sentimental value', and this time she intended to take immediate action. No one was to leave the dining hall and, while they waited there, the staff were going to search all the rooms and dormitories.

'This is not something we're undertaking lightly,' Miss Allen said. 'All of you have a right to privacy, and we respect that. But you have a more important right, and that's to know that your money, your possessions, and ultimately you yourselves, are safe while you're in the school's care.'

The four friends looked at each other.

'Johnny!' signed Spike, and Jess shook her head.

'Wonder what those photos of sentimental value were,' murmured Ash.

'Probably Shannon in her bikini,' said Foxy, but nobody managed a smile.

The students finished their lunches and sat at the tables, drinking cup after cup of tea and watching the rain fall outside. At intervals, teachers led small groups to the toilets across the quadrangle. An hour passed, then two. Conversations flared up, and then, equally swiftly, died away. There was nothing, really, to talk about. Everyone prayed that the searches would provide an answer to the mystery and an end to the atmosphere of distrust. At the same time everyone dreaded what that answer might turn out to be. Would the thief turn out to be a friend? A room-mate?

Finally Miss Allen marched back into the dining hall. Within seconds, the place was silent.

'Thank you,' she began. 'You've all been very patient. We've finished for now, so please go quickly and quietly to wherever you're meant to be.'

At first no one moved or spoke. Then there was the sound of chairs being pushed back and a sudden, excited buzz of conversation. Had the staff found something?

Jess and her friends returned to Room 10 and had barely sat down when someone knocked at the door. It was Miss Harper, one of the first-year singing teachers.

'Ashanti?' she said. 'I've just come from the school office. Could you pop over there and speak to Miss Allen?'

Ash stared at her, wide-eyed. 'Did she say what it was about?'

'Just that she needs to speak to you.'

'Er . . . OK,' said Ash, darting a mystified look at Jess as she pulled on the wet rain jacket that she'd taken off just minutes earlier.

They watched her go. 'She was in that dance class when Flick's money went missing,' said Foxy. 'Maybe they want to ask her about that.'

Jess nodded. 'Or maybe it's nothing to do with all that. Maybe there's, I dunno, some problem at home or something.'

Spike, who was sewing ribbons on to a new pair of pointe shoes, kept her thoughts to herself.

Half an hour crawled past, and then there was another knock at the door. Jess and Foxy jumped and Spike, seeing their reaction, looked up. It was Miss Harper again, and this time the message was that they should all go to the school office.

'Why do I have the feeling this is gonna be bad?' murmured Foxy as they crunched across the wet gravel drive behind the singing teacher.

'Could be anything,' replied Jess, trying to ignore the fear rising inside her. 'They're probably talking to all sorts of people.'

'I hope so,' breathed Foxy. 'I really, really hope so.'

Miss Harper held the front door open, then followed the three girls into the main building. In the outer office Mr Dye, the school secretary, was tapping away at his keyboard. Jess and her friends were among his favourite students, but today he didn't give them so much as a twinkle. Mungo was more welcoming and, seeing Spike, he sat up in his basket with a whimper of pleasure.

Miss Allen looked up as they came in. She was standing by the window, her back to the fading afternoon light. Opposite her, Ash was sitting in an armchair, staring unblinkingly ahead.

'OK, girls,' Miss Allen began, taking her place behind the desk. 'I'm afraid this isn't going to be easy. As you know, we were forced to take the unpleasant step of searching all your rooms this afternoon. I asked Miss Harper to take charge of your floor. And this is what we found.'

Jess leant forward, a sick feeling rising inside her. On the desk were a worn leather wallet and a small blue cardboard box.

'Johnny Finn reported his wallet missing this morning,' Miss Allen continued. 'And this, as I'm sure you'll recognize, belongs to Shannon Matthews.' She opened the box. Inside, twinkling on a bed of tissue paper, was the crystal bracelet.

'I found them both in Ashanti's drawer,' said Miss Harper quietly. 'The money from the wallet was missing.'

The room seemed to grow darker. Beside her, Jess could hear Spike's agitated breathing. Ash, meanwhile, went on staring straight in front of her, her eyes unblinking.

'She didn't take those things,' said Jess. 'Someone put them there.'

Miss Allen peered over the top of her glasses. 'But, Jessica, why would anyone do that?'

'I don't know. To make it look like Ash took the money, not them. But I promise you, she isn't a thief.'

'Jess is right,' said Foxy. 'Whoever stole that wallet and that bracelet, it wasn't Ash.'

'She hasn't denied taking them, Eleanor,' said Miss Allen quietly.

Foxy stared at Ash in disbelief. 'Tell them,' she said. 'Just tell them you didn't do it.'

Ash didn't move, but a tear began to slide down her cheek.

'Ash,' said Foxy desperately. '*Tell them!*'

Spike walked forward and, falling to her knees in front of Ash, began signing urgently. Ash ignored her, and when Spike took her hands she turned her head away.

Miss Harper took a step forward. 'Verity. I think . . .'

'She can't hear you,' said Foxy coldly. 'She's deaf.'

Miss Allen threw a despairing look at Jess, who went over to Ash and Spike. 'I know you didn't do this,' she whispered to Ash. 'So please. Speak up now. For all of us. Please.'

But Ash said nothing, just continued staring in front of her as the tears rolled down her cheeks. Gently, Jess disengaged Spike's hands from Ash's and led her back to where Foxy was standing.

Miss Allen shook her head. 'Ashanti, I'm very, very sorry it's come to this. But I'll have to send you home until further notice. Do you three girls have anything else to tell me? Any other information to offer?'

One by one, they shook their heads.

'All right then. I'll tell you what's going to happen. Miss Harper will take Ashanti back to her room now and help her pack. And you three, Jessica, Eleanor and Verity, will go into Reading with Mr Huntley, to help with the arrangements for the Christmas pantomime. Verity, I know you're not in it, but I'd like you to go along too.'

For a moment none of them spoke. 'Can we say goodbye?' Foxy asked.

'Yes,' said Miss Allen. 'Do it now.'

Hesitantly, they went over to their friend and took it in turns to hug her.

'I'm so sorry,' Ash whispered. 'I just didn't have any choice.'

'About *what*?' hissed Foxy.

'Forget it. Doesn't matter. None of it matters.'

Jess and Spike were close to tears now, but Foxy wasn't. Foxy was pale with anger. She stood up, her flame-red hair swinging round her face, and turned to Miss Allen.

'You're making a *big* mistake here,' she hissed. 'I don't know what's going on, but this girl has never stolen anything from anyone, and we're gonna prove it.'

Miss Allen frowned. 'Eleanor, you're upset, and given the circumstances I'll ignore your inappropriate tone. Now could the three of you please wait in the outer office. Mr Huntley will be here shortly.'

They trooped out. A few moments later, Miss Harper led Ash past them and out of the building.

Mr Dye glanced at the three of them sympathetically as he polished his reading glasses, which hung round his neck on a gilt chain. He was a large man, who years ago had worked on TV talent shows. Like Miss Allen, he still had something of the backstage manner about him.

'So,' he said eventually. 'Ashanti's going home?'

Jess sniffed and nodded. Spike, crouching by Mungo's basket with her face buried in the dog's neck, didn't see him speak.

'You know what happened?' asked Foxy, her face still taut with anger.

'That Jayne – Miss Harper – found some of

the missing bits and pieces in her drawer? Yes, I was here when she came in to report it.'

'There's been a mistake,' said Foxy. 'Something weird's going on. Ash isn't a thief.'

Mr Dye frowned thoughtfully. 'Maybe, even if that's the case, it's better that she's out of the way for the moment?'

Jess and Foxy looked at him uncertainly.

'Look, I've worked at Arcadia for more than ten years, and in all that time I have never seen Miss Allen take a decision that wasn't in the best interest of the school and the students. She is not a cruel person. Trust me, she will discover the truth, one way or another.'

'If she doesn't, we will,' said Jess.

'Fair enough, but promise me you'll watch how you go. Don't throw wild accusations around the place; that won't help Ashanti or anyone else.'

'So you believe us?' asked Foxy. 'That someone else put those things in her drawer?'

'Right now, I have no idea what to believe. But here's a suggestion. If you have any suspicions, bring them to me first, OK?'

'Deal,' said Foxy grimly.

'Excellent. And now, ladies, right on time, here's Mr Huntley to take you to Reading. Nice little house, the Theatre Royal. You'll like it.'

18

Sitting in the van with Spike and Foxy, the windscreen wipers thumping away and Mr Huntley playing Kiss FM on the radio as if nothing had happened, Jess felt wretched and helpless. She knew, as they all did, that Ash would never steal from anyone. It was simply not in her character. So what were that bracelet and wallet doing in her drawer? *And why hadn't she denied having anything to do with it?*

Looking at Foxy and Spike, Jess could see that their thoughts were going round and round in the same circles as her own. Meeting her eye, both of them shook their heads in bewilderment.

'Perhaps one of us should get in touch with Zane,' Foxy said. 'I'm guessing Ash won't have had the chance to let him know.'

'Shouldn't we let her text him or whatever?' Jess said, and Spike nodded her agreement.

The three of them looked at each other warily.

Mr Huntley was the friendlier sort of teacher and knew Jess and Foxy well from singing class, but they still had to be careful what they said in front of him. A dark thought, though, had lodged in Jess's mind. And she was pretty sure that Spike was thinking the same thing. They settled back in their seats, exchanging the odd furtive glance, and watched the wet suburbs of Reading crawl past.

The Theatre Royal was a red-brick Victorian building, once grand, but now shabby. The stage door was in a shopping precinct, next to a cafe. Inside, in a tiny office, an elderly man was stubbing out a roll-up cigarette in a tin ashtray. Mr Huntley spoke to him briefly and he leant towards a microphone.

'Mr Scott to the stage door, please.' The message echoed tinnily through the building, and soon a man with a whiskery, ferret-like face arrived. Roger Scott was dressed in a brown corduroy suit and a cravat and seemed overjoyed to meet them, shaking each of their hands in turn and asking them to call him Scotty.

It turned out that Scotty would be directing *Cinderella*, and as they followed him and Mr Huntley up the stairs the three girls looked around at the yellowing posters, the naked light bulbs and the threadbare carpet. Soon they were in the half-dark of the backstage area. Around them was a confusion of electrical fittings, divided by black curtains. To one side, by a piece of painted scenery, someone was arranging costumes on a rail.

After a few more steps, light poured over them. They were standing on the stage, which sloped gently down towards a line of brass footlights. Below these they could see the orchestra pit and rows of plush crimson seats receding into the dimness.

Gazing out into the auditorium, seeing the dim gleam of the brass rail at the front of the dress circle, Jess felt an electric jolt of recognition. She didn't care if the backstage area was shabby because here, where it mattered, everything was perfect. For more than a hundred years, actors had stood on this stage, feeling the same thrilled challenge rise up inside them.

Beside her, the director smiled. 'Yes, this is where the magic happens.'

'What's on at the moment?' Jess asked.

'*Charley's Aunt*,' said Scotty. 'We're lucky enough to have Aubrey Charles with us. Do you know his work at all?'

'Um . . . not really,' admitted Jess, who hadn't heard of the play.

'Old-school classical actor,' said Scotty. 'People still talk about his Hamlet. Especially Aubrey.'

They stood there for a moment and then followed him off the stage. As they made their exit through the wings Jess thought of Ash, driving home in tears, and was sure Foxy and Spike were thinking of her too. In silence, they followed the director up another short flight of stairs to the backstage canteen, where a large, shiny-faced woman was poring over *Heat* magazine.

'And this is the lovely Joan,' announced Scotty. 'By far the most important person in this building.'

Joan looked up suspiciously. 'What d'you want then?'

'What do any of us want? Immortality, I suspect . . . But for now, my proud beauty, we will settle for tea and cake.'

Joan moved heavily towards a steaming urn, rolling her eyes. 'Go on then, sit yourselves down. I'll bring it over.'

The three girls installed themselves at a table beneath a framed poster for a production of *The Wind in the Willows*. Beside them Scotty and Mr Huntley discussed travel arrangements for the pantomime. After a short time Joan came over, swiped the crumbs off the tabletop and on to the carpet with a greying dishcloth, and plonked mugs of brick-red tea in front of them. A moment later she followed these up with large slices of bright yellow cake. Both were delicious.

'The minute we're back, we get to work proving that Ash is innocent,' said Jess. 'We can't wait; the longer she's away, the harder it'll be to find anything out.'

'I agree,' said Foxy. 'Spike?'

Spike nodded.

'And I think we should get some help,' Jess continued. 'You might think this is kind of weird, but I suggest we involve Shannon.'

'Why?' signed Spike, frowning. 'She's a total –'

'Look, I know. Shannon's a lot of things. But she's not a liar, and she's not a thief. She's smart, and she probably knows what's going on in Arcadia better than anyone.'

'And why do you think for one moment that Shannon Matthews would want to help us?' asked Foxy. 'Why should she care if Ash is suspended, or even expelled?'

'Because, like I said, she's smart,' said Jess. 'She may not care about Ash, but she knows her well enough to be sure she'd never steal anything. Shannon had her bracelet taken and, um . . .'

'Johnny?' asked Foxy delicately.

Jess nodded. 'Yeah, he had his wallet taken. Shannon'll want to know who was responsible for that, I guarantee it. She'll want revenge.'

'Don't think we should involve Johnny,' signed Spike with an apologetic glance at Jess.

'No,' said Foxy. 'He's not trustworthy.' She turned to Jess. 'Sorry, babes, but that's the truth.'

'No, you're right,' said Jess, and something shifted inside her. Johnny Finn *wasn't* trustworthy, she realized. She'd known this for some time, but somehow it hadn't mattered. Now, with Ash's career in the balance, it mattered a great deal.

She was musing on this when the door swung open and two men sauntered into the theatre canteen, one with wild hair and a silvery beard, the other bullish and ruddy-faced.

'In thirty years in this profession,' the silvery beard was saying, 'I have never, *ever* been spoken to like that. I said to her: *My dear young lady, when I was playing Hamlet . . .*'

'Remind me again, Aubrey. Where *was* that?' enquired the ruddy-faced man, winking at Jess, who was openly staring at them.

'British Council tour, Cyprus, 1978. Myself, Coral, Ian, Judi . . . Night after night, pin-drop silence. Two teas and a Kit Kat please, Joan, my love. Of course, you couldn't begin to assemble a cast like that today.'

'Of course not.'

'Who, today, can speak the verse?'

'Who indeed?'

Although mesmerized by the pair, Jess dragged her attention back to her friends. Fired by a sudden resolve, she linked arms with Foxy and Spike. 'We're going to sort this thing out,' she said. 'We're going to find out who stole that money and rescue Ash.'

'Deal!' said Foxy. 'Now who's gonna ask Joan for some more of that delish cake?'

19

'Love what you've done with the place,' said Shannon.

She looked around Room 10 without enthusiasm. At the ageing *Twilight* and *Hunger Games* posters, the little ballet shrine on Spike's chest of drawers, the stacks of playscripts, sheet music and schoolbooks, and the bedcovers heaped with dance wear and sports kit. The only halfway tidy area was Ash's, now unbearably emptied of her things. Even her bed had been stripped, and Shannon had the decency to pause for a second or two before lowering her Hollister-jeaned backside on to the mattress cover.

'So,' she said. 'Talk to me. What do you want?'

'Ash didn't steal that money,' said Jess. 'We want you to help us find out who did.'

Shannon thought for a moment and nodded. 'You're right about one thing. That little princess hasn't got what it takes to be a thief.'

Foxy narrowed her eyes but said nothing.

'Oh please,' Shannon murmured. She turned to Spike. 'And you too, Sugar Plum. I'm not afraid of you, so you can stop giving me the evils, yeah?'

Spike's eyes widened, and her hands fluttered angrily.

Shannon smiled. 'I don't speak deaf and dumb but I'm guessing that means "get her out of here". Am I right?'

No one moved.

'Obviously I am.' She stood. 'OK, you got it.'

'Wait,' said Jess, and, jumping up from her bed, she blocked the way to the door. 'Please . . . Stay.'

For a moment the two of them stood there, face to face. And as she looked into Shannon's sapphire-blue eyes, framed as they were by those photo-perfect features, Jess saw something unexpected. A kind of loneliness. The knowledge that the tough, independent course she steered through life left her with few real friends. *She envies me*, Jess realized. *She thinks herself superior to me in every way – looks, confidence, talent – but still she envies me.*

Later, Spike would tell Jess that she and Shannon had stood there eyeballing each other for just a few seconds. But to Jess it felt as if they stood there forever. And somehow, by the end of it, each of them knew exactly what the other was thinking.

Biting her lip, Shannon turned round and took her place on Ash's bed. 'OK, take that scene again. Where were we?'

'I'll make some tea,' said Jess.

'That would be good,' said Shannon, pulling her cardigan round her shoulders. 'It's ten degrees colder down this end of the corridor.'

'The thing I'd like to know,' said Foxy, 'is why. Why this person needs money so badly they're prepared to risk being expelled to get their hands on it.'

'*She's* prepared to risk it,' said Shannon. 'It's got to be a girl. Most of it's happened in this block. Any boy would be spotted immediately.'

'Boys do occasionally make their way up here,' said Foxy. 'But you're right. They are kind of visible.'

'And our thief doesn't take risks,' said Shannon. 'She's too smart for that. She sees her chance and takes it.'

Spike fingerspelt a name.

Jess and Foxy looked at each other. 'She says, do you think it could be Kelly?' asked Jess.

Shannon smiled. She knew there was no love lost between Spike and Kelly. 'Actually, I wondered that,' she said. 'I worked out that it would have been just about possible for her to do the first thefts. But on the morning that Johnny's wallet was taken from the theatre Kel was in bed at the other end of this corridor with some stomach thing, heaving her guts up. Disgusting, actually, but it definitely wasn't her.'

'What about Flick?' asked Jess. 'Did anyone actually see that fifty-pound note she said was taken from her pocket in Miss Pearl's class?'

The perfect lips twitched. 'You've got a sneaky mind, Bailey, I must say. But FYI, yeah, I did. It came that morning. It was her birthday, and the money was from her dad, and she was going to use it to buy one of those make-up kits, with all the toners and moisturisers and stuff. And then by lunchtime she'd lost the money and was in this total state. Mental. Trust me, if it was either of those two, I'd know.'

After handing out the tea, Jess perched on the end of her bed, mug in hand. 'Can I make a suggestion? What we need to do is look at each theft and make a list of who was around at the time. Take that dance class where Flick had her money stolen. If we assume it had to be someone in that class, then we're already down to a dozen people. Spike, why don't you find out who was there that morning? And, Foxy, if I talk to Emma, could you speak to Ricky about his iPod and who was in the area when that went missing? And Shannon? Your bracelet and Johnny's wallet? Because if the same name keeps cropping up . . .'

She looked around the room. Spike and Foxy nodded.

Shannon smiled, showing her sharp little teeth. 'This could be interesting! I have a feeling we're gonna end up with a very short list indeed . . .'

20

Spike, Georgie and Paige started rehearsals with the English National Ballet two days later, taking an early train from Pangbourne. Spike had been deeply upset by the Olly business – 'It's amazing just how unhappy you can feel about something that never happened,' she told Jess – but suddenly she became her old self again, her smile as wide and her fashion sense as extreme as ever.

The rehearsal days were long and demanding – Clara was a major role, and she and Giselle were involved in almost every scene in the ballet – and Spike arrived back at the school aching and exhausted. But it was wonderful, she told Jess, her eyes shining. Vladimir, having seemed grumpy at the audition, turned out to be the kindest and most patient of teachers, and Juliet Dale was lovely too.

Best, though, were the other dancers, who immediately recognized Spike as one of their own. Her deafness very quickly stopped being an issue. Accustomed to expressing themselves physically rather than in words, her new colleagues instinctively found ways of making themselves understood to her. At least a dozen nationalities were represented in the company, and during breaks in rehearsals Spike would find herself lip-reading snatches of conversation in Spanish, Portuguese, French and Russian. Working across language barriers was second nature to the dancers, and communicating with Spike became a game which she enjoyed as much as they did, and which made her feel accepted and valued.

And there was a mischievous light in her friend's eyes that suggested to Jess it wasn't just the dancing that had put such a spring in her step. There was a boy in the production whom Spike mentioned increasingly often. His name was Alexei, he was a scholarship student from St Petersburg in Russia, and he was sixteen. Alexei was dancing the role of Clara's brother, and he spoke barely a word of English.

Which made things 'kind of interesting', Spike dryly informed Jess. She and Alexei made themselves understood by a mixture of play-acting and texting, with one of the other Russian dancers acting as interpreter. Anxious to get the full story on this possible romance, Jess questioned Paige.

'They're very sweet together,' Paige confirmed. 'Kind of circling round each other like cats. The whole company's watching to see what happens.'

'So is he good-looking?' Jess asked.

'Are you kidding? He's off-the-scale *gorgeous*. His feet, oh my god. And his *arabesque*!'

'Paige, I'm sure he's ballet-gorgeous, but is he guy-gorgeous?'

'Totally! I'm well jel.'

'Fingers crossed then.'

'You bet,' said Paige.

21

Emma Tucker shared a room with Poppy Rattigan and Emilia Bell. They were a strikingly different trio. Emma had tumbling brown hair and a big voice; Poppy was all legs and freckles; and Emilia was a sporty, rather ordinary-looking girl until you saw her speaking lines on stage and realized that you couldn't take your eyes off her.

Jess had timed her meeting with Emma for mid-afternoon, so that Emilia was at netball practice and Poppy had a ballet class with Miss Pearl. Now the two of them faced each other. It was bitterly cold outside; Emma had a thick sweater zipped up to her nose and Jess, as the guest, had been invited to wrap herself in Poppy's duvet and sit by the radiator.

She explained to Emma that she and the others didn't believe Ash had stolen anyone's money or possessions and that they meant to find out who had. Emma agreed that Ash seemed the last person to take anything from anyone and promised to help. She told Jess how, on a Thursday morning the previous month, her mother had sent her a letter with fifty-five pounds folded inside it. 'Two twenty-pound notes, a ten and a five,' she explained. 'I'd earned it doing this sponsored walk during the summer holidays, and the idea was that I would give it to Miss Allen, so that it could go towards one of the school charities. I got the letter at breakfast and opened it in the dining hall. Lots of people saw because Mum also sent a photo of Norah, my rat, and I was, like, showing that round.'

'A lot of people saw the money?'

'Quite a few. I mean, I didn't hide it. I was quite pleased with myself, it had been hard earning it, I'd walked eleven miles on a really hot day, and it never occurred to me that anyone would, you know, *steal* it. I mean, I know Flick lost that money and Shannon's bracelet had gone missing but . . .' She shrugged. 'Stupid of me, I guess, but you know how it is. Anyway, I brought the letter up here and put it in that top drawer there. What I meant to do was give the cash to Mr Dye after lunch, but I forgot because there was a netball match that afternoon and I was the A-team wing attack. I came up here afterwards but I didn't think about the money, and by the time I remembered, after supper that evening, it had gone.'

'Everything?'

'No, the letter was still there, and the photo of Norah. And obviously all my socks and stuff, he didn't take those!'

'He?' said Jess.

'I mean, like, whoever.'

'But why did you say he?'

Emma looked confused. 'I don't know. I guess I just thought of the thief as a he.'

'Funny, because Shannon's sure it's a girl.'

'Look, Jess . . . this is just between us, yeah?'

'Uh-huh.'

'You know Johnny comes up here in the day sometimes, to see Shannon?' She looked away. 'Sorry, perhaps you didn't.'

'Emma, trust me, the whole me-and-Johnny thing is so over.'

'Really?'

'Really truly. History. Like the Tudors.'

'OK, well, like I said, Johnny comes up here. And sometimes Zane comes with him.'

'So what are you saying?'

'Just that . . . Look, OK, a couple of days before Johnny's wallet went missing and Ash was sent home, I found Zane wandering around this corridor. He looked kind of weird and I asked what he wanted and he said he was there with Johnny, visiting Shannon and the others. But Shannon and Kelly and Flick's room is right up the other end, so I thought it was strange.'

'Yeah, definitely. But how do you mean that he was looking weird?'

'Kind of . . . pleased with himself. Like he had a secret. Something no one else knew.'

'And you didn't say anything to anyone?'

'Well, he is a friend of Johnny's and Shannon's. And boys are allowed to visit during the day, so . . .'

Jess frowned. 'But you're saying he was quite often in this block during the day. For no obvious reason?'

Emma nodded slowly. 'I guess I am, yeah.'

'But you didn't see him up here on the day you lost your money?'

'No, but then I was playing in the match all afternoon, and so was Emilia, and Poppy's always off with her ballet gang, so . . .'

'And you didn't see him here on the day the wallet and the bracelet turned up in Ash's drawer?'

'No. But again, I wasn't here most of the time.' Jess nodded.

'Look, I'm not accusing him or anything,' said Emma. 'I'm just saying.'

'I hear you,' said Jess.

22

After tea, leaving the dinner hall, Jess caught up with Shannon. To begin with the other girl was friendly enough, but when Jess asked her about Johnny and Zane she was immediately defensive.

'What are you suggesting?' she asked. 'That the two of them have been going from room to room, robbing people?'

'Look, all I'm asking is how often they've visited you in our dorm block,' said Jess, scrunching up her toes in her shoes to keep them warm.

'This term, I suppose Johnny's been up perhaps eight to ten times,' said Shannon, her voice muffled behind her scarf. 'And Zane's come with him maybe three or four of those times. Look, can we get indoors? I'm frozen.'

Jess nodded and led the way through the half-dark to the dorm block and the comparative warmth of the locker room. It was lit by a single yellowish bulb, and the faint, muddy smell of sports kit hung in the air.

'This is nice,' said Shannon, wrinkling her nose.

'It's private,' said Jess, seating herself on a low bench and leaning back against the battered metal lockers. 'And here's the thing. Do you remember the day that Johnny's wallet went missing?'

'Er . . . yes,' said Shannon, lowering herself to the bench opposite Jess. 'It was a Thursday.'

'Did Johnny and Zane visit you here on the Tuesday? Or earlier that week at all?'

'No. If he comes over here, or both of them do, it's Friday evenings or weekends.'

'Because Emma said she saw him wandering about "looking weird" on the Tuesday. And he was up our end of the corridor, nowhere near your room.'

'Well, maybe he was visiting Ash. I know you're not very familiar with the whole boyfriend– girlfriend thing, Bailey, but it does happen. And the two of them were kind of an item.'

'I know that. And I also know that Ash would have told the rest of us if she'd had Zane in our room.'

'Really?' said Shannon. 'Are you sure about that?'

'Yeah. We don't hide stuff from each other.'

'Aww. How sweet. Except that's not how life works, Jessica. People have secrets. They have lives other people don't know about.'

'She would've told us,' insisted Jess.

'Maybe,' said Shannon, getting to her feet. 'And maybe not.'

23

Back in Room 10, Jess practised her sign language with Spike for half an hour, and then went to the office to collect Mungo, as it was her turn to take him for his final walk of the day. As she and the dog crossed the lawn, which was already hardening with frost, Jess took the opportunity to rehearse a speech from *Romeo and Juliet* that she'd been learning for Colette Jones's class.

'*Come, gentle night . . .*' she recited, Mungo panting quietly at her side, '*Give me my Romeo; and, when he shall die, take him and cut him out in little stars . . .*'

Tears sprang to her eyes. She had a pretty good idea how she'd act the part; she and Juliet were both fourteen, after all. But would she ever meet anyone she could love as completely as that? Would the night ever give her a Romeo of her own?

Unleashing Mungo, she watched as he raced away and was swallowed up in the darkness of the woods. What, she wondered, made some people act as they did? Her mum, for example. Was she incapable of happiness? And if so, had she, Jess, inherited the same curse? Was she doomed to go through life alone? At that moment, as she stood there on the frosty lawn, leash in hand, it seemed like a very real possibility. 'You love me, don't you?' she said sadly as Mungo bounded back to her. 'But then you love everybody, so that doesn't count.'

Suddenly seized by the desire for a chocolate-chip cookie, or perhaps three, Jess made her way back to the dorm block, dropping the dog off on the way. In Room 10 she found Foxy waiting for her return, so they could ring Ash.

When it was Jess's turn to speak, she asked her if Zane had ever been up to Room 10.

'I never asked him up there,' Ash answered. 'That time he brought me the rose, we went to the locker room to talk. Why do you ask?'

'We're just trying to, y'know, run through all the possibilities,' said Jess warily.

'Well, I'm trying not to think about all that stuff. I've got my Phoebe Skye audition tomorrow.'

Jess closed her eyes. The audition! *Of course* . . . No wonder Ash sounded tense. She forced a smile. 'Really, *really* good luck for that, babes.'

'Thanks. Don't forget about me, will you?'

'As if! We're totally gonna prove you innocent.'

'Yeah, well . . . You all sound so far away.'

'Trust us, babes. We're here for you. Spike sends love.'

'OK, give her a hug from me. Missing you all. Bye.'

'Bye.'

Thumbing the Disconnect button, Jess felt empty. And guilty of making promises she couldn't possibly fulfil. How could they hope to prove their friend innocent? There were close to a hundred students at Arcadia, all coming and going at the same time. How could they ever establish who had been where at the time of all the thefts? They'd been mad to think it was possible.

That night, the wind rose, whipping through the bare boughs of the trees outside and making the Room 10 windows shudder. Cocooned in pyjamas and duvet, Jess was almost asleep when she heard the beep of her phone.

> U awake?
>
> Mmm . . .
>
> Can't sleep 4 thinkin bout Ash
>
> I know ☹
>
> Feel def, stupid, useless

No!!

Wish I cd help more :/

All doing r best . . . How's Nut?

Gr8

Alexei??

☺

?

WE KISSED!!!!!!

OMG Tell!! :o

Walked me to the bus then . . . !!!

Woo-hoo!!!

Xactly ;)

So does he speak Eng yet?

No!

???

We manage :P

OMG! OMG! OMG!!!

I know! * sighs *

Well good 4 u babes go 4 it!!

Yep u bet ;)

C u tmoz xx

Tmoz xx

24

The next morning, without Ash to set her usual example, the three of them lay huddled beneath their duvets as the minutes ticked past.

'There's ice on the windows!' groaned Foxy. 'What is this? The fourteenth century?'

Jess could see she'd have to be the sensible one. Dragging herself out of bed, she shook Spike, and then switched the lights on. Five minutes later they were all more or less dressed except Foxy. 'Has anyone seen my pink sweater?' she wailed. 'I can't find it anywhere?'

'Lend you one?' suggested Spike, but Foxy was very particular about her clothes, and Spike's weird charity-shop knitwear wasn't her thing at all.

'I know it's in here somewhere,' she muttered, hurling clothes out on to her bed. 'Yes, there you are . . .' From the very bottom of her dance bag, she pulled out the sweater and, as she did so, something fell to the floor. An envelope.

'*To My Beloved* . . .' read Foxy. 'Oh. My. *God*. Someone's sent me a love letter.'

'Open it!' ordered Jess.

'*To the most beautiful girl in the world. I will heart you till the stars go out* . . . Aw, that's so *sweet*!'

'What else?' demanded Jess.

'Nothing else,' said Foxy dreamily. 'But, hey, isn't that enough?'

'So who's it from?' signed Spike. 'Who put it there?'

Foxy shook her head. 'No idea. Could be anyone. I haven't cleared this bag out for, like, *ages*.' Her gaze softened. 'Perhaps . . .'

'No, it is *not* from Mr Casey,' said Jess, staring at the letter. 'Apart from anything else, he'd have spelt it right.'

'How d'you mean?'

'Well, he wouldn't have called you the most beautiful *gril* in the world, even if he thought you were. Which he doesn't.'

'Well, *somebody* hearts me,' said Foxy. 'Even if I am only a gril.'

'And you're not the only one,' said Jess. 'Somebody hearts Spike too.'

'Cool!' said Foxy. 'Who?'

'My ballet partner, Alexei,' Spike signed demurely.

'He kissed her at the bus stop,' said Jess.

'Oh, babes!' breathed Foxy. 'That's so romantic. It's like that TV series, what's it called? *Anna Karenina!* Tell me *everything.*'

'Over breakfast,' said Jess firmly. 'Come on, you grils. I'm starving.'

Outside, the temperature was close to zero and, as the three of them hurried towards the dining hall, the lights from the school buildings glimmered on the frozen puddles.

'Seriously,' muttered Foxy, 'who d'you think sent me that note?'

'Seriously, I have no idea,' replied Jess, her eyes watering with the cold. And Spike slowly shook her head.

Over breakfast, they discussed Spike and Alexei's kiss, and picked over the love-note mystery, but without getting any nearer discovering Foxy's secret admirer.

'So no one's been looking at you in that "I'll die if you don't snog me" kind of way?' asked Jess, washing down her bacon sandwich with a gulp of tea.

'Well, obviously boys *look*,' said Foxy. 'I am, after all, the mysterious Eleanor Fox. But no one in *quite* that way, no.'

When they left the dining hall, the sky had cleared to a hard, icy blue. The exact same shade as Johnny Finn's eyes, Jess noted, without even a twinge of regret. How fast those feelings faded! One day a boy was your whole life, the next he was just . . . a boy.

As the three of them crossed the drive, Jess saw a grey shape appear at the corner of the main building. It was Mungo, out for a morning walk with Calvin and, seeing his beloved Spike, he bounded towards her. With her head turned towards Foxy, Spike neither saw nor heard the big dog approaching.

When he cannoned into her, she was crossing a patch of black ice. As her legs flew from under her Jess saw her friend's eyes widen with shock. Spike threw an arm out, then her wrist seemed to crumple beneath her and she smacked into the hard ground.

For a split second, no one moved except Mungo, who, pleased with this new game, began to lick Spike's face. Then Calvin ran up and pulled the dog away, desperately apologizing as Spike, gasping with pain, tried to roll her body away from her injured wrist.

'Don't move,' said Foxy, pulling off her track top and easing it beneath Spike's head. She and Jess tried to gather icy gravel to pack round Spike's wrist, but it was frozen solid.

Sending Calvin to find Miss Pearl, Jess angled herself so that Spike could see her face. 'Can you wriggle your toes?' she asked, to make sure there was no serious damage to the other girl's back. Like all Arcadia dance students, she knew what to do in the event of a bad fall.

Spike nodded, her face colourless. She was shivering now and biting her lip. Other students gathered round, laying their own track tops over her in an attempt to keep her warm. Then Miss Pearl arrived and took charge. Ten minutes later Spike was on her way to hospital. Helpless, Jess and Foxy watched her leave.

'I'm really sorry,' said Calvin, who had just returned Mungo to the office. 'I should've kept him on the lead. I forgot that Verity couldn't hear him.'

'It wasn't your fault,' said Jess.

'Well, thanks . . .' He hesitated. 'And sorry for . . . that stuff I said about you. I didn't mean it. About you thinking that you –'

'Calvin, it's OK. Forget it, really.'

'Thanks, Jess.' He backed away, smiling self-consciously, then swung round towards the boys' dorm block.

'I think he's over you,' murmured Foxy.

'I think you're right,' said Jess.

Spike was back by midday, her wrist heavily bandaged and in a sling. Miss Pearl brought her up to Room 10, where Jess and Foxy were preparing to go down to lunch. Spike was very pale and barely looked at them. Instead she lay down on her bed, her arm at her side.

'They've taken X-rays,' Miss Pearl said.

'*Nutcracker?*' asked Jess.

Miss Pearl shook her head. 'Not for the time being, I'm afraid. And if that wrist's badly sprained, or even broken, not this year.'

Seeing Spike lying there like a wounded bird, Jess's heart went out to her. Taking her friend's good hand, she gave it a squeeze.

'She'll be OK,' Foxy told Miss Pearl. 'We'll look after her.'

'All right,' said Miss Pearl. 'You do that and, please, keep that wretched dog away from her. Verity, dear, I'm going now.'

Spike nodded and turned her face to the wall. Jess sat with her and said nothing, because there didn't seem to be anything to say. Then she and Foxy pulled on their coats and scarves and went down to lunch.

25

That evening, as Spike lay on her bed with the *Nutcracker* music whispering from her iPod, Jess and Foxy skyped Ash. As the two of them huddled round Foxy's laptop screen, their friend's super-tidy bedroom came into view, followed by Ash herself.

'I didn't get the Phoebe Skye gig,' said Ash. 'I made it to the last four and they took the other three.'

'Oh no!' said Jess. 'That is so . . .'

'It's how it is,' said Ash tonelessly. 'I just wasn't good enough, full stop. And since I'm probably not coming back to Arcadia, I wanted to tell you guys something. The first is . . .' She blinked and was silent for a moment. 'The first is to thank you for being the best friends I've ever had, and ever will have. And the second thing . . . well, I'm only going to tell you the second thing if you promise not to tell anyone.'

'We promise,' said Foxy, after a short pause.

'I didn't take that money. I would never, ever steal anything from anyone.'

'We know that,' said Jess.

'I'm afraid it was Zane. The day before that stuff turned up in my drawer, he told me he'd been up in our room.'

'Go on,' said Foxy.

'He said he'd left something for me to find. Something that would tell me how he felt about me. I didn't know what he meant. And then, when they searched the room, they found Shannon's bracelet and Johnny's wallet . . .'

'So *that's* why you wouldn't say anything to Miss Allen,' said Foxy. 'You thought he'd stolen it for you.'

'I didn't know what was happening. But I knew that if I said anything Zane would be in serious –'

'But, Ash,' Jess cut in, 'how much worse does it get than expulsion?'

'Much worse.' She hesitated. 'Truth is he's been in trouble before. With the police, I mean. He told me that before he went to Arcadia he was pretty wild. There were problems at home but he was also quite dyslexic, which no one spotted. He couldn't keep up with the work so he started missing school, and he was soon running with this crowd of older boys who were, like, *really* bad news.'

She sniffed and hesitated for a moment.

'Anyway, one day a bunch of them got caught shoplifting clothes and Zane was charged. He hadn't stolen anything but he was there and none of the others spoke up for him. In the end they just gave him a police warning, but that was a couple of years ago. He's fifteen now. If he gets a conviction for theft he could go to a Young Offenders Institution. And that's like . . . prison.' She was crying now, trying to blink away the tears.

'But, Ash,' said Foxy gently, 'you can't sacrifice your whole career for him.'

'What career? I have no career. And Zane's not . . .' She sniffed again. 'He just had a *really* tough start in life and . . . I don't know, I . . .'

'If it *was* him, and you don't say anything, he'll just go on doing it.'

'Jess is right,' said Foxy. 'You totally have to speak up.'

Ash shook her head. 'I can't do that to Zane. And you've promised me you won't say anything either. Best thing is if I just stay away.'

'Ash, please!' said Jess. 'Think about this.'

'I've thought about nothing else. Now I gotta go. Love you guys. Give Spike a hug from me.'

And she was gone.

26

The next day, after morning classes, Jess and Foxy made their way to the room Shannon shared with Kelly and Flick. It felt strange to be there, seeing Shannon's clothes strewn about and smelling the scent of her Victoria Beckham perfume. It was funny, thought Jess. Three of them shared the room, but the only personality that came through was Shannon's. Where the others had pin-ups of pop stars above their beds, she had portraits of herself and one or two with Johnny. *Say what you like about Shannon Matthews*, Jess mused, *the girl knows where she's going.*

'So where are we?' asked Shannon. 'How's our detective work going?'

Jess glanced at Foxy. Both of them, she was sure, were asking themselves the same question: was there any point to the investigation now that Ash had told them about Zane?

Maybe there is, thought Jess, *and maybe there isn't.*

Ash was obviously sure in her own mind that Zane was the thief, but nothing that she'd said actually proved it. There was still an outside chance it could be someone else. Either way, they'd given their word to Ash that they wouldn't tell anyone what she'd said, and now, for better or worse, they were bound by it. They just had to carry on as if the previous night's Skype conversation had never taken place.

'We've got our lists,' said Foxy, holding up three sheets of paper. 'I spoke to Ricky Purkiss and worked out who might have had the chance of stealing his iPod, Jess talked to Emma, and Spike got Miss Pearl to show her the class register for the morning that Flick's money went missing.'

'Well, we've made progress too,' said Shannon.

'We?' said Jess.

'I got Kelly and Flick to help,' said Shannon airily. 'You didn't think I was going to do the whole thing myself, did you? Anyway, we've made a list of everyone we think could have been around when my bracelet and Johnny's wallet were taken. So now I suggest we put all those lists together and see if any names crop up on all of them.'

Foxy laid her lists down on Shannon's chest of drawers, just as Flick and Kelly walked in. Seeing Jess and Foxy, they stopped dead.

'Meet the investigating committee,' said Shannon with a faint smile.

'Right,' said Flick, dropping her bag to the floor. 'So where's the twinkle-toed Miss Nash?'

'Spike couldn't come,' said Jess.

'Injured, I hear?' said Kelly with a smirk. 'Something to do with that dog you guys brought back from London?'

'She's hurt herself, yeah.'

'Mm. Too bad.'

'Come on, people, concentrate,' said Shannon. 'I'm going to read out the longest list, that's the me-and-Johnny one, and if I read out a name that's on all the other lists, then we underline it. That way we'll have a shortlist of everyone who was around for all the thefts. Anyone got a better idea?'

No one had, so they set to work, with Flick and Kelly exchanging whispered comments on the sidelines. Five minutes later they had their shortlist. It consisted of just four names:

Emilia Bell
Johnny Finn
Ashanti Taylor
Zane Johnson

For a long moment, they all just stared. Then

Shannon shook her head. 'Sorry, but no way. I don't think it's any of them.'

'Why not?' asked Kelly.

'Emilia and Ash because they couldn't. Johnny and Zane because they wouldn't.'

Flick frowned. 'I guess Johnny's not about to steal his own money. But I'm not sure I'd rule out Zane.'

'And why's that exactly?' asked Shannon.

'Opportunity,' said Flick. 'I've lost money, Johnny's lost money, you've lost your bracelet. And Zane's always been, like, *around.*'

Kelly nodded. 'And with apologies to you guys –' she turned to Jess and Foxy – 'I don't find it so hard to imagine Ash being involved either. I mean, face it. That stuff was found in her drawer. If you ask me, she and Zane were in it together.'

Jess closed her eyes. Why had Shannon chosen to involve Flick and Kelly? It was impossible to think clearly, with the two of them throwing random accusations around. Although when it came to Zane perhaps they weren't so random.

'Shannon, we really need to think about this, OK?'

'I agree with you, Bailey. We do.'

'What's to think about?' asked Kelly. 'I vote we take these lists to Miss Allen right now.'

'No one asked for your vote,' said Shannon,

and Jess saw the other girl's eyes narrow with resentment.

'Like Jess said, we need to think,' said Foxy, getting to her feet. 'Let's give it twenty-four hours.'

'You've got it,' said Shannon. She yawned and shook her blonde hair. 'Flick, I'd like that blue top back, please. I want to wear it this afternoon. Could you iron it for me?'

'Yes, Shannon,' said Flick with a sideways glance at Kelly. 'Of course!'

Out in the corridor, the Room 10 girls looked at each other.

'That was all just a little too weird,' said Foxy.

'You're not kidding,' said Jess.

27

Jess was worried about Spike. The X-ray had shown that her wrist wasn't broken, but it was badly sprained, and whether or not she would be able to continue in *The Nutcracker* depended on the outcome of a second hospital visit. For the time being the company were rehearsing with Ayako taking the role of Clara in her place.

For some reason, Spike had convinced herself that her wrist would not heal in time and that she would not be allowed to continue with the rehearsals. Giselle kept her updated on the production and texted her regular get-well messages, but these didn't seem to help. And there was no word from Alexei.

Despite their usual closeness, Jess couldn't get through to her friend. Unable to sign and unwilling to text, Spike lay on her bed for hours at a time, staring into space. Even discussing Ash and the thefts seemed beyond her, and when Jess and Foxy tried talking to her she listened and nodded but didn't really engage with them.

'She's depressed,' said Foxy as the two of them walked back from Mr Huntley's singing class the next day. 'I guess we don't realize how hard it is for her. Just keeping going day after day, trying to keep up with the academic work, trying to follow what everyone's saying, trying not to seem different . . . Her dancing keeps her going, and if that's taken away from her, her world starts to break down.'

'We just have to be there for her,' said Jess. 'And hope that her wrist heals, so she can get back to rehearsals.'

Foxy nodded. 'The person we do need to talk to, though, is Zane.'

Jess frowned. 'We promised Ash we wouldn't say anything.'

'It's gone beyond being just between him and Ash. Face it, Jess, he's our thief. And the only way we'll get Ash back is by making him admit it.'

'OK, but I think we should ask Spike first.'

'You think so? She doesn't seem very interested in all that right now.'

'We're in this together, Foxy. We always have been.'

'I guess you're right.'

Back in the room, they explained the situation to Spike, who agreed they should speak to Zane, but felt, like Jess, that they shouldn't mention what Ash had told them. 'We made her a promise,' Spike signed. 'We can't break it.'

'So where are we going to meet Zane?' asked Foxy.

'Green room?' suggested Spike. The others agreed, and Foxy texted him.

He answered five minutes later. Clearly mystified, he agreed to meet them after lunchbreak.

'I'm not looking forward to this,' said Jess.

'Gotta be done,' said Foxy, and Spike nodded her agreement.

The rest of the morning crawled past. Spike went to the dining hall with the others at lunchtime but ate almost nothing. Instead she stared blankly into the middle distance, hip hop hissing from her earphones.

Jess watched her friend with concern. 'You have to build up your strength,' she told her. 'And you're not going to do that with an apple and a pot of yoghurt. How is your wrist, anyway?'

Unhurriedly, Spike paused her music. Then she flexed her wrist experimentally and shrugged.

'It looks better,' said Jess. 'You need to tell Miss Pearl and get back into class.'

'OK, Mum,' Spike signed, with the ghost of a smile.

'I mean it,' said Jess severely. 'All this lying

around moping isn't doing you any good at all. When's that doctor supposed to decide about you doing *Nutcracker*?'

'Tomorrow.'

'Well, you tell him or her that it's fine, and then you go into rehearsals and take your role back, OK?'

Slowly, Spike nodded.

'Good,' said Jess. 'Now go and get some of that sticky toffee pudding. At least two scoops.'

'Jess, go easy on her,' said Foxy as Spike hesitantly rose to her feet.

'No, I won't go easy,' said Jess. 'I'm not going to sit back and watch that role slip away from her. She's got to fight for it, and if she hates me for telling her that, then tough.'

Foxy shook her head, amused. 'Listen to you, Jess. It's just your second term, but sometimes I think you're the most Arcadian of all of us.'

'I just know that we need each other if we're going to survive,' said Jess.

Foxy watched Spike as the Scottish girl warily approached the pudding counter. 'You're right,' she said. 'But don't forget to save some of that fighting spirit for yourself.'

Jess shook her head. 'Don't worry. Behind this sweet and caring mask, I'm pure Shannon Matthews.'

Foxy grinned. 'Just checking.'

28

'No way!' said Zane. 'Absolutely *no way*. I mean, I wanna see Ash back here as much as anyone else. More than anyone else. But I did *not* steal that stuff, and I'm not gonna tell Miss Allen I did.'

Jess looked at the others. She and Spike were perched on the threadbare sofa, Foxy had her legs drawn up beneath her in an old armchair, and Zane was sitting on the radiator. The green room smelt, as usual, of theatrical make-up, musty costumes and dust.

Foxy shook her head. 'Look, Ash definitely didn't do it. And you were, like, around when every one of those things went missing. The cash, Shannon's bracelet . . . all sorts of people said they saw you in our dorm block.'

'Yeah, well, I had my reasons to be there. Which didn't include stealing anything, I give you guys my word.' He looked at them one by one, his gaze unblinking. 'Look, Jess, we're friends, right? Who was there for you last term when half the school was calling you a B.I.T.C.H. for gettin' too close to Johnny Finn?'

'You were,' said Jess. 'That's true. And I'm grateful for that, really. But right now we're trying to save Ash's career.'

'Yeah, well, you won't do that by ruining mine. You know how I feel about Ash and, if you want me to help you find out who stole that stuff, I'm here. But it wasn't me. On my mother's life, guys. *It was not me.*'

Spike waved her good arm to attract their attention. 'I don't think we're getting anywhere with this,' she signed.

'What's she say?' asked Zane.

Foxy translated.

'And she's right,' said Zane. 'I'm sorry, people, I just can't help you. I'm not your thief. You better keep looking.' And with that he slid from the radiator and walked out of the green room.

For several seconds no one spoke or moved. Then both Jess and Foxy turned to Spike. From experience, both of them knew how good she was at reading people by their body language. By the way they sat, stood and moved their faces.

'I really don't know,' signed Spike. 'But I think I probably believe him.'

'What about all that stuff Ash said!' protested Foxy.

'She *definitely* thinks it's him,' added Jess.

Spike nodded and shrugged. All of them were thinking the same thing. If they were wrong, and it wasn't Zane, then who was it?

Spike's phone vibrated in her pocket. As she read the text message, her expression changed. Slowly, her smile grew wider and wider. She stared at the screen for a moment, biting her lip, then passed the phone to Jess.

> Veraty, you arm mend yet? New girl not so beutiful dancer like you!!! Come back quick!! Alexei xx

Jess grinned at her and, reaching across, took her hand. Spike blinked, her eyes shining.

'Bad news?' asked Foxy, concerned.

Spike smiled, shook her head and burst into tears.

In the dining hall, an hour later, Jess sat staring at her tea. It had been a long term, and it looked as if it might end with Ash expelled and the mystery of the thefts unsolved. There was the pantomime to look forward to, but, although rehearsals started in less than a week, it seemed part of some far-distant future. Would her mum be there to see it, Jess wondered. There had been no reply to her last email, so she concluded, sadly, that she wouldn't.

She was happy for Spike, though, who suddenly seemed her old self again. At intervals, when she thought no one was watching, she would glance at Alexei's text message and a dreamy, faraway look would overtake her. After the meeting in the green room she'd done a full ballet class, the first since her injury, and her wrist had given her no trouble at all. All that she needed now was the go-ahead from the doctor, who was coming the next day. If he decided that her wrist was up to it, she would be allowed to return to the *Nutcracker* rehearsals. *Fingers crossed*, thought Jess, who knew how devastated Spike would be if the decision went against her.

Slowly, the dining hall began to fill, as students drifted in for a drink or snack to keep them going through the long afternoon classes. Vaguely, Jess noted Emma join the queue for the tea urn with Linnet, who was bobbing her head to the rhythm of the song on her iPod. Flick and Kelly stood a few places behind, and then there was Calvin, who seemed to be gazing at Linnet.

'That boy's definitely moved on,' murmured Foxy.

'Yes, it –' Jess began, but then fell silent, feeling the pressure of Spike's fingers on her arm. From a distance, the Scottish girl's face would have looked expressionless, but Jess could see the intense, unblinking concentration in her eyes.

What had she seen? Was it Johnny at that far table, diamond ear-stud flashing as he flirted with Emilia, who seemed much more interested in her playscript? Was it Mr Casey, running his fingers through his fringe as he engaged Ricky and Olly in earnest conversation? Was it Paige or Georgie, their arms flying as they argued over some obscure point of ballet? Spike's grip tightened, so that Jess could feel her fingernails digging into her arm through the sleeve of her track top.

'What is it?' Jess murmured, but Spike, her face pale, shook her head. Beside her, Foxy raised a questioning eyebrow, and Jess gave the faintest of shrugs.

Zane came into the dining hall, his face troubled. Beside him, Shannon seemed to be nodding sympathetically. A moment later she slipped away and moved up the queue to speak to Flick and Kelly. *Placing her tea order*, thought Jess. *Why on earth do those two put up with it?* Zane and Shannon then sat down at a table next to Johnny, who quickly turned away from Emilia.

Gradually, Spike's grip on Jess's arm relaxed, and her eyes lost their distant focus. 'I know who stole all that stuff,' she signed. 'And I know why. We've been wrong about everything.'

'Go on,' said Foxy.

And Spike did. And as she continued – slowly, so that there should be no mistake – Jess and Foxy's faces paled too, and their mouths fell open.

'Oh my God,' whispered Jess. 'That is just . . . awful.'

Foxy pulled out her phone and thumbed a number. 'Listen,' she said, her voice expressionless. 'We need to talk.'

29

Silently, the girls crossed the lawn in single file. Foxy led, followed by Shannon, Kelly, Flick, Spike and finally Jess. The frost was powdery underfoot and glittered sharply beneath the full moon.

From the lawn they followed the path through the woods, the lights of the school fading behind them. Still no one spoke; the only sounds were the occasional snapping of twigs and the distant hooting of an owl. For a time they were almost enclosed by darkness and the skeletal limbs of trees, and then the clearing opened out before them, silver in the moonlight. One by one, they carefully descended the icy amphitheatre steps to the stage area.

'So,' said Kelly, looking around her, her face invisible beneath her hood. 'I'm guessing you have some news on the thefts.'

'I've just spoken to Ash,' said Foxy. 'I've told her she can expect to be back here within twenty-four hours.'

'That's great!' said Flick, stamping her feet. 'But why did you bring us all down here to tell us? I mean, please! I'm *frozen*.'

'No one will interrupt us here, that's why,' said Jess.

'Ok*aaay*,' said Kelly. 'But why the secrecy? If Ash is coming back, everyone's gonna know, right?'

'Ash is coming back because she didn't take any of those things she was accused of stealing,' said Shannon. 'My bracelet, Ricky Purkiss's iPod, Emma and Johnny's money . . .'

'You're forgetting my money,' said Flick.

'I don't think so,' said Shannon, folding her arms.

'What do you mean?'

'That money never went missing. You just said it did.'

For a moment the six of them stood there, unmoving.

'And why would I do *that*, Shannon?'

'Because you figured that when other stuff started to go missing you wouldn't be suspected. You or Kelly.'

'You're totally nuts,' said Flick, as Kelly turned to stare at Shannon, open-mouthed. 'You're saying the two of us stole all that stuff? Why would we do that? I mean, your bracelet, for example. Why?'

'So you had something to plant on Ash that made it look as if she was the thief. Money wouldn't have worked; it had to be something recognizable. Everyone knew that bracelet was mine.'

'Sorry, Shannon, but you've got this way, *way* wrong,' said Kelly.

Shannon met her gaze. 'In that case, can you explain the conversation you were having in the dining hall an hour ago, when you were discussing stealing Georgie Maxwell's new phone?'

'When we were *what —*'

'Let me remind you. You said you reckoned you could get three hundred pounds for it on eBay, and Flick said, *But, hey, wait a minute, now that everyone thinks Ash stole the other stuff, wouldn't it spoil things if anything went missing when she wasn't there?* And you said, *I know, I thought of that, but it may be our last chance, and three hundred pounds takes us past our target . . .'*

'What *is* this?' hissed Flick. 'Who told you we said *a single word* of this stuff?'

Shannon put her hand on Spike's shoulder. 'Guess who? She lip-read your entire conversation.'

Flick looked from Shannon to Spike and back again, her face marble-white in the moonlight.

'What I really want to know,' said Shannon, 'is *why*. What did you want all that money for?'

Kelly stared at her, her features sharp with defiance. 'You *really* wanna know?'

'Shut up, Kelly,' said Flick, her voice steady.

'No, I'm not going to shut up,' said Kelly. 'It's about time she knew what other people really thought of her.'

'Don't,' said Flick. 'Just say nothing and walk away. You think anyone's going to listen to what *this one*' – she nodded at Spike – 'thought she lip-read in the dining hall? I don't think so. She made it all up.'

'And why would she do that?' asked Foxy.

'Because she's *jealous,* obviously.'

'Of what, exactly?' asked Jess.

'Of *us*, Bailey. Sure, she can dance, but who wants to spend their life slaving away in ballet class? We can sing, we can act, and when it comes to looks . . . I mean, please! When did a boy last give this skinny freak a second look?'

Spike ignored her, but Jess started forward, so angry that, for a moment, she didn't know what she was doing. And then Foxy's hand closed tightly on her wrist.

'So tell me,' said Shannon to Kelly. 'Tell me what people think of me. I'd be interested to hear.'

'Don't,' said Flick. 'She's just –'

'No,' said Kelly. 'It's time she heard it. She thinks she's so great, ordering the two of us about

192

as if we're, like, her personal shop assistants – *get my sweater, Kelly; fetch my shoes, Flick* – but you know what? You're *mean*, Shannon. A really, really *nasty* person.'

'Kelly,' said Flick, a warning tone in her voice. 'That's enough, OK?'

'No, please,' said Shannon. 'Go on. This is getting interesting.'

Flick started to walk away. Then she turned back. 'You think you're so awesome, don't you, with your modelling contract and your fashion shoots? Well, I've got news for you, Shannon Matthews. We have agents too. Fashion shows, magazine work, everything. We're gonna be *very* busy.'

'Good for you,' said Shannon. 'Who's taken you on?'

'HeatWave. It's one of the big agencies. Get used to it, Shannon. You've got competition.'

Shannon smiled. 'Er, no. I don't think so, actually. I know the names of all the big model agencies, and HeatWave isn't one of them. Where are their offices?'

'They're, like, online.'

'Ah, so you haven't been there.'

'We don't need to, Shannon. That's not how it works any more. We emailed them our pictures and they took us on. And they've got a *lot* of work lined up for us.'

Shannon nodded slowly. 'Just as soon as they've put your portfolios together, right?'

'Yeah, obviously.'

'And how much is that costing you?'

'None of your business,' said Flick. 'Kelly, let's go.'

'Just let me get this right,' said Shannon. 'You found a model agency online and emailed them some pictures. They then answered saying that you were perfect for modelling and they could get you lots of work. First, though, you had to put a professional portfolio together that they could show clients. So they asked you to send, what? Two hundred and fifty pounds each? Three hundred? Something like that? For the photographer?'

Flick reached for Kelly and tried to steer her away, but Kelly stood frozen to the spot, her eyes fixed on Shannon.

'I'm right, aren't I?' said Shannon. 'And of course you didn't have that kind of money, so you decided to steal it. And, boy, were you smart! Saying you had that cash taken from your tracksuit during class. Who would suspect you after that? Plus of course your dad sent you another fifty quid. Clever stuff. And from then on the two of you worked together, covering for each other and making sure you were never in the same place when anything went missing. Like my bracelet – taking that must have felt *really* good – and Ricky's iPod, which I'm guessing went on eBay. And then more cash from Emma and Johnny, until bit by bit you get the money together. And, to cover yourselves, you plant my bracelet and Johnny's wallet in Ash Taylor's drawer to make it look like she was the thief. Classy, guys. Really classy.'

Flick stood there in the moonlight, blank-faced. Kelly, meanwhile, had started to shake. With fear or the cold, Jess couldn't tell.

'And you know what?' Shannon continued. 'It was all for nothing. That "model agency" rip-off is the oldest trick in the book. They told me about it when I joined Tempest. You set up a website, make up a name like, say, HeatWave, and tell everyone who applies that they're perfect, whatever they look like. So then you've got a steady stream of wannabes, all desperate to become models, all sending in hundreds of pounds for photo sessions, which turn out to be five minutes with some sleazy guy in a rented studio. They don't even process the pictures because of course there's no real agency, and there certainly won't be any work.' Shannon shook her head. 'If either of you knew the first thing about modelling you'd know two things. One, that no decent agency would take you on without meeting you face to face; and two, that you never, *ever* pay for photographs.'

No one moved. Flick and Kelly stared at Shannon, and Shannon stared right back.

'Sorry,' she continued. 'But I absolutely guarantee that you're never going to hear from HeatWave again. You've turned this school upside down, upset everyone, and got a girl who never did you the slightest harm expelled. And all for . . . nothing.'

There was a long silence.

'You can't prove a word of this,' said Flick.

'I think most people in this school would probably believe us,' said Foxy. 'And I expect the police would be interested to hear that HeatWave, whoever they are, have been taking money from fourteen-year-olds.'

Flick stared at her, no longer able to hide her fear.

'The alternative,' said Shannon, 'is that you both go and see Miss Allen first thing tomorrow morning and tell her everything.'

'Get Ash back here,' said Jess. 'That's the main thing.'

This time the silence seemed to last forever. But finally Flick nodded, and Kelly did the same.

30

By teatime the next day, Flick and Kelly were gone. What arrangement they'd made with Miss Allen, no one would ever know. But the room they had shared with Shannon had been cleared of their things, and new class lists and timetables had been printed and pinned to the school notice board – lists in which there was no mention of Flick Healey or Kelly Wilkinson. Another newly printed notice announced that Ashanti Taylor and Poppy Rattigan had joined the cast of *Cinderella*.

'I think the deal is that if she helps me with my tap dancing I'm supposed to do something about her singing,' said Ash.

'Poppy's singing makes me sound like Rihanna,' said Foxy, taking a thoughtful bite of a chocolate biscuit. 'You've got quite a job on your hands.'

'On the other hand, Ash is *definitely* the world's worst tapper,' signed Spike with a grin.

'Yup, it's great to be back,' said Ash, surveying the busy dining hall. 'Wow, have I ever missed you guys.'

'It's been insane,' said Jess. 'Just the weirdest time. To begin with, there was the whole thing with Spike's wrist.'

'I know, you told me about it. Mungo!'

'It was me,' signed Spike. 'I didn't see him coming.'

'Yeah, well, either way. What a scare,' said Ash.

'I know. I really thought the whole *Nutcracker* thing was . . .' She slid a finger across her throat. 'But then this morning the doctor in Pangbourne checked it out and said it had healed well enough for me to go back to rehearsals on Monday.'

'That's so great.'

'I know. And I just got a text from my friend Giselle too.'

Decided 2 pay u visit! R u free tmoz? How do I get RKdia?? Xxx

'Wow!' said Jess. 'That's nice of her.'

'We could take her to that tea shop in Purley,' said Foxy.

'What did you answer?' asked Ash.

Gr8! CW2CU!! Get train 2 Pangbourne then bus. Hope u like cake xxx

Spike put the phone back in her pocket. 'I'm really sorry about Phoebe Skye,' she signed.

Ash shrugged. 'I did my best. So, you know, whatever.'

'There'll be other auditions,' said Foxy. 'Don't worry, you're going to be a huge star one day.'

'Huge is what I'm gonna be if I go on eating cake at the rate you guys do . . . But you won't care, will you?' she asked, reaching out a hand to Zane who, freshly showered after a dance class, had just taken his place beside her.

'What about?'

'What size I get.'

'Well . . . we'll have to see. There are limits.'

'I hate you,' sighed Ash.

'No, you don't.'

'OK, maybe not totally.' She turned to Jess. 'Tell me again about the whole money-stealing, modelling thing. I still can't *believe* what those girls did.'

'I know,' said Jess, stirring her tea. 'It was just so . . . sad, really. And it completely tore the school apart. No one believed you were the thief, by the way. Not even Shannon. In fact, especially not Shannon.'

'No,' said Zane. 'You thought it was me!'

Jess closed her eyes. 'I feel really bad about that. We all do.'

'Well, it *was* kind of weird. But I guess I can see how you got there.'

Ash grinned. 'Tell us again what you were doing all those times. Hanging around our corridor like that.'

'You know what I was doing. Trying to get that note to you.'

'That note saying . . . What, exactly?'

Zane gave her his goofiest grin. 'That I will love you . . . until the stars go out.'

'And that you're the most beautiful gril in the world,' added Foxy.

'And so, genius that you are, you stuffed the note into Foxy's dance bag,' murmured Ash.

'Well, it was on your bed.'

Ash rolled her eyes.

'I suppose you know that it broke my heart to find out that note wasn't for me,' said Foxy.

'Tell us,' said Jess. 'How is that nice Mr Casey these days?'

'Put it like this: I don't think he's quite ready to commit.'

'Really!' said Ash. 'Why ever not?'

'Well, for a start, he still doesn't know my name. He called me Helena this morning in improv class.'

'Yes, I noticed that,' said Jess.

'I mean, do I *look* like a Helena? I thought that was very hurtful.'

'I agree,' said Jess. 'Especially after all those natural disasters you've lived through together.'

'Well, quite. And, to be honest, I think I can do better.'

'I'm sure you can. A smart, attractive gril like you.'

31

The next morning, Jess jumped out of bed early and, making sure not to wake the others, pulled on her tracksuit and trainers for a run. Outside it was still half-dark, but a wintry dawn glow was spreading through the sky.

Setting off across the frost-pale lawns, she reflected on the events of the past weeks. The atmosphere caused by the thefts had been horrible, and even though she felt a measure of sympathy for Kelly and Flick – living in Shannon's shadow can't have been easy – she was glad they were gone. With the mystery solved, the school had seemed to breathe a collective sigh of relief.

A few weeks earlier, Jess remembered, she had been running in the pouring rain. At the time, she'd been in such a state about Johnny. Now she was over him, pure and simple. *How did that work,* she wondered. *How could you care so much one day and not the next?* Perhaps she should ask Calvin, who in the last week or so seemed to have completely lost interest in her. Now he was following Linnet around, gazing after her with that sad, longing expression of his.

Ahead of her, beyond the lawns, the grey shapes of oaks and beeches strained against the wind. Running towards them, Jess wondered if she had made any progress at all this term. Perhaps, although it often didn't feel like it, and dance and singing were still a struggle. Acting, though, she loved, even if it did mean spending hours learning lines. It was the thrilling strangeness of becoming someone else. That sense of stepping into a new body that looked like your own but wasn't, at least not quite. Because when you were in it you were untouchable. The character wasn't you, so you couldn't be hurt. And, because you couldn't be hurt, you could take the maddest risks.

She was in the woods now, skeletal branches overhead, frosted leaves and icy puddles underfoot. And here was the clearing and the amphitheatre where the final act of Flick and Kelly's deception had been played out. And now the woods again and the red-brick towers of the main building just visible through the tree trunks.

When she got back to Room 10 Spike was pulling on her tights for Miss Pearl's Saturday morning class, which was aimed at the handful of students who were destined to become professional ballet dancers. After the cold air outside, the room felt unnaturally warm. In their beds, Foxy and Ash slept on.

'What's the weather like?' signed Spike.

'Chilly,' Jess replied, plugging in the kettle, and Spike smiled as she zipped up her track top. The click of the door behind her was not loud, but it woke Ash, who sat up, blinking.

'Hi, babes,' said Jess. 'Tea?'

Ash frowned. 'Did you know a cockroach can live on a single grain of sugar for a month?'

'So can some models, apparently.'

'Urrgh.'

'Sorry, won't mention models.'

'Please don't.'

Foxy stirred and opened one eye. 'What's going on?'

'It's a new day!' said Jess.

'Oh God, no!' groaned Foxy. She hauled herself wearily on to one elbow. 'I was having this dream. I was in Pangbourne and this huge tidal wave was rushing up the High Street. Then I saw Mr Casey running towards me.'

'Did he save you?' asked Jess.

'No, he totally drowned . . . Are you making tea?'

Two hours later, the four room-mates were

waiting for Giselle in front of the main building, the wind flattening their clothes to their bodies. 'Hope she's not going to be *too* long,' said Foxy, shifting from foot to foot, and Jess, her hands thrust deep into the pockets of her hoodie, hoped much the same.

'She's super-organized,' signed Spike, her nose pink above her turquoise scarf. 'She won't be late.'

As they stared up the drive towards the school gates, Jess heard the door of the main building open and close behind them. It was Miss Pearl, deep in conversation with Paige and Georgie. From the opposite direction, meanwhile, came Olly, with Mungo trotting obediently beside him. All of them came to a halt as a car nosed between the gates and made its way slowly down the drive, its taxi light shining a dim yellow. The car came to a halt and Giselle stepped out. There was someone with her, a male figure, his face invisible as he turned to pay the driver.

The car pulled away and the figure straightened. Fair-haired and, with the easy grace of a panther, he was by far the best-looking boy Jess had ever seen.

Releasing Jess's arm, Spike began to walk towards him. Slowly at first. And then, when he saw her and smiled, she flew to him, throwing her arms round his neck. For a long moment, as they held each other, there was an amazed silence, which was broken by Ash letting out a triumphant whoop, swiftly echoed by Paige.

Eventually Alexei put Spike down, gently kissing the tip of her nose. They grinned shyly at each other and, hand in hand, followed Giselle towards Jess, Ash and Foxy.

'Now *that's* what I call romantic,' murmured Jess. She caught Giselle's eye, and the Royal Ballet School girl smiled her catlike smile. Glancing at Olly, Jess saw that he looked pleased for Spike too.

'Am I imagining things,' said Ash, 'or is Miss Pearl looking distinctly teary?'

'You're imagining things,' said Foxy. 'Teachers don't cry.'

32

In the girls' chorus dressing room, the temperature was rising. The heating in the Theatre Royal seemed to have been set to stone cold for the weeklong rehearsal period, but this afternoon, for the first time, the old iron radiators were blasting out waves of heat. Sitting at her place between Ash and Foxy, Jess felt her muscles tingling beneath her dressing gown. An hour earlier, in preparation for the opening matinee, Poppy Rattigan had given them all an extra-thorough warm-up on stage. As dance captain, she took her responsibilities seriously.

Peering forward into the long mirror, Jess inspected her make-up. Her reflection gazed back at her, dark-eyed beneath the lights. *I'll do*, she thought.

To her left, Ash was going through a similar routine. 'What do you think?' she asked Jess, dusting her cheekbones with dark peach blusher. 'Cover girl or clown?'

'Looking good,' said Jess.

To her right, Foxy snapped her flame-red hair into a ponytail. 'I think our parents are sitting together,' she said to Ash. 'I made sure it wasn't *too* near the front.'

'Thanks,' said Ash. 'That tap number's complicated enough as it is; I'd rather not be staring straight at them. When did you say your dad was coming, Jess?'

'He gets back from Saudi next week,' said Jess, sliding a final kirby grip into her hair. 'I'm not sure exactly when he's coming to see the show.'

Foxy lined up her lipsticks in front of the mirror and, after some thought, selected one. 'I think, given the occasion, it's got to be the Chanel Rouge Coco Paradis,' she announced.

Ash smiled. 'Guess who's determined to be the most glamorous tap-dancing mouse in Berkshire.'

Above the dressing-room door, the speaker crackled. 'Half-hour call, please, ladies and gentlemen. This is your half-hour call.'

Swinging round in her chair, Jess checked that all her costumes were hanging on the rail, each with its matching pair of tap, jazz or pointe shoes, that her satin mouse-tail was securely fastened to her costume, and that her mouse-ears and whiskers were hanging by their elastic from the back of her chair.

There was a knock on the door. 'Are you decent, ladies?'

It was Roger Scott, the pantomime's director, in a wine-red velvet suit. He was carrying a bouquet of pink roses. 'Break a leg, my lovelies. I know you're going to be fabulous.'

Pacing the length of the dressing room, he gave each of them a rose. 'Emilia, Poppy, Emma . . .'

'Thank you,' said Jess, when it was her turn. Each stem, she saw, was fitted with its own little test tube of water. The pink petals smelt, very faintly, of expensive soap.

'I'm going out the front in a minute, we've got some local press in, but I just want to say thank you. You've worked really hard – now go out and have fun!'

The director was followed by a parade of other visitors, all making the ritual opening-day round of the dressing rooms. The popular *EastEnders* actress who was playing Cinderella, despite the fact that her fortieth birthday was long behind her. The two Ugly Sisters, both men in grotesque make-up and wigs. The former boyband member who was playing Prince Charming. And Aubrey Charles, who was playing Baron Hardup, Cinderella's father. '*A king of shreds and patches*,' Aubrey announced with mournful pride, indicating his costume. 'And which of you young ladies knows where that quote's from?'

'*Hamlet*,' the six girls answered in unison. They'd heard quite a lot about *Hamlet* in the last week. But for Jess it had been fascinating to watch such an experienced actor preparing a role. Much of the pantomime was very silly indeed, with lots of clowning and terrible jokes. But, as Aubrey and the other principals demonstrated, making the silliness work was a serious business.

'It's a hard world out there,' Scotty had told them on the first day of rehearsals. 'And what we're offering people is the chance to escape it. To be transported, like Dorothy in *The Wizard of Oz* –' (they'd heard quite a lot about Dorothy too) – 'into another, magic world. And it's your job, with every step you dance, and every word you sing, to make that world real. It doesn't have to make sense, but it does have to come from the heart.'

Aubrey was the girls' final visitor, and when the door had closed behind him Ash stood up. 'OK, guys,' she announced. 'It's that time again. We need to warm up our voices.'

'This is your revenge for all those tap corrections, isn't it?' groaned Poppy as they all got to their feet.

'You bet!' said Ash. 'And here we go. Standing straight, breathing out . . .'

Ten minutes later, they were done and, tucking her mouse-tail into the back of her tights so that it wouldn't drag on the floor, Jess slipped from the dressing room.

Outside, a tatty strip of carpet led to the boys' dressing room. Halfway along it was a staircase down to the stage, and a small window overlooking the street. On the other side of the dingy glass it was snowing, the whirling flakes white against the slate roofs and the grey of the sky. Two floors below, people jostled as they queued for admission to the warmth of the theatre foyer. From above, Jess could see the vapour of their breath, the feathery snowflakes settling on their hoods and umbrellas, the tickets held in their gloved hands. A small girl in a blue windcheater looked up, saw Jess at the window and pointed excitedly upwards, pumping at her mother's arm. Smiling, Jess waved at the little girl. *Just a few years ago*, she thought, *that would have been me. Thrilled to bits to catch a glimpse of the backstage world.* And now this other dimension was where she lived.

Stepping away from the window, Jess reached into the pocket of her dressing gown and took out an envelope with a Saudi Arabian stamp and an airmail sticker on it. Inside was a handwritten letter.

My darling Jess,

I am writing rather than emailing because this is strictly between you and me. I have two pieces of news. First, that Elaine has been offered a senior teaching post at McGill University in Canada. It's a fantastic job, and she never intended to stay for more than a year in Saudi. She told me that she would renew her contract here and turn down the McGill offer if I wanted her to. But I didn't feel that I could ask her to do that. I'm fond of her, and I think she is of me, but as I told her, that's not enough to justify the sacrifice of her career. So she has said that she intends to accept. There are no hard feelings between us and she wishes you the very best of luck. She wanted me to tell you that your Titania, at the end of last term, was one of the finest student performances she'd ever seen.
So there you go.

My second piece of news concerns Mum. As you may or may not know, it's all over between her and Derrick. He has worked his way through all her savings, and for the last few months she has been working as a waitress in a hotel in Durban, where she's also been living. Her intention is to return to London as soon as she has the price of an air ticket. I offered to pay for her but she refused, and she expects to be here early in January. To begin with, she will be staying at your Aunt Rena's. What this means for us all, it's too early to say, except that hopefully your mother will be part of your life again. As for her and me – we've agreed to meet, but that's as far as it's gone. It's been a difficult and painful time for all of us, and we shall have to take things one step at a time. So let's see. You say that the theatre has promised you a pair of tickets. I'm hoping that she returns from South Africa in time for us to come and see you in Cinderella *together. Again, let's see.*

In the meantime, my love, have fun in the pantomime. I'm sorry I won't be seeing more of you over Xmas, but I know you'll be having a wonderful time. Say hi to your room-mates.

Your loving Dad xxx

Reflecting for a moment, Jess returned the letter to its envelope. What the future held she didn't know, but right now it was the present that mattered. She looked out of the window but the little girl was gone. She and her family would be in the foyer now, stamping the snow off their feet, folding their coats, hurrying to take their seats. And, seeing the thickening white swirl outside, Jess felt a rush of happiness so sudden and unexpected that she gasped and placed a hand over her heart.

Everything's fine, she told herself. *And that's enough.*

As she turned away, still light-headed, the five-minute call came over the tannoy. Looking down the stairs, she saw the door to the boys' dressing room open and Olly and Ricky step out, laughing. Jess watched them for a moment, and then Olly glanced up and saw her. She gave him the ghost of a wink, and he smiled back.

Back in the dressing room, Ash handed Jess her whiskers and ears. The others were standing now, tense and expectant in their costumes.

Familiar and not familiar, thought Jess. She glanced in the mirror, and at first wasn't sure which dark-eyed figure was her, and which was Foxy and Emma and Emilia. *Whichever*, she thought.

Poppy looked at them and grinned. 'OK, you mice,' she said, looping her tail over her arm. 'Tap shoes on, and let's knock 'em dead.'

Stars

Enter the
Arcadia School of
Performing Arts at
www.stars-books.co.uk
and . . .

- Discover more about the books and the authors
  - Meet Jess, Foxy, Ash and Spike
 - Enter cool comps and play quizzes and games
  - Find top tips on how to become a STAR
 - Sign up and be the first to get all the Stars goss

The Arcadia School
of Performing Arts –
where dreams are made
and stars are born . . .

It all started with a Scarecrow

Puffin is over seventy years old.
Sounds ancient, doesn't it? But Puffin has never been
so lively. We're always on the lookout for the next big
idea, which is how it began all those years ago.

Penguin Books was a big idea from the mind of
a man called Allen Lane, who in 1935 invented
the quality paperback and changed the world.
**And from great Penguins, great Puffins grew,
changing the face of children's books forever.**

The first four Puffin Picture Books were hatched in 1940 and the
first Puffin story book featured a man with broomstick arms called
Worzel Gummidge. In 1967 Kaye Webb, Puffin Editor, started the
Puffin Club, promising to **'make children into readers'**.
She kept that promise and over 200,000 children became devoted
Puffineers through their quarterly instalments of *Puffin Post*.

Many years from now, we hope you'll look back and
remember Puffin with a smile. **No matter what your age
or what you're into, there's a Puffin for everyone.**
The possibilities are endless, but one thing is for sure:
whether it's a picture book or a paperback, a sticker book
or a hardback, **if it's got that little Puffin
on it – it's bound to be good.**